N/O

N/O

NON OZ

Ron Silliman

ROOF BOOKS
NEW YORK

Portions of these two poems were first accepted for publication by *Caliban,
Columbia Poetry Review, Conjunctions, Croton Bug, Hot Bird Mfg, Ironwood,
Margin #4/Period(ical), New American Writing, Object Permanence, Screens and
Tasted Parallels, Southpaw, Sulfur, Talisman,* and *Tyounyi.* My thanks to the editors for their support of my work.

Volumes containing portions of *The Alphabet*
>   ***ABC***, Tuumba, Berkeley, CA, 1983
>   ***Demo to Ink***, Chax Press, Tucson, AZ, 1992
>   ***Jones***, Generator Press, Mentor, OH, 1993
>   ***Lit***, Potes & Poets Press, Hartford, CT, 1987
>   ***Manifest***, Zasterle Press, Tenerife, Canary Islands, Spain, 1990
>   ***Paradise***, Burning Deck, Providence, RI, 1985
>   ***Toner***, Potes & Poets Press, E. Hartford, CT, 1992
>   ***What***, The Figures, Great Barrington, MA, 1988

Other books by Ron Silliman
>   ***Crow***, Ithaca House, Ithaca, NY, 1971
>   ***Mohawk***, Doones Press, Bowling Green, OH, 1973
>   ***Nox***, Burning Deck, Providence, RI, 1974
>   ***Ketjak***, This Press, San Francisco, CA, 1978
>   ***Sitting Up, Standing, Taking Steps***, Tuumba, Berkeley, CA 1978
>   ***Legend*** (with Bruce Andrews, Charles Bernstein, Ray Di Palma and
>   Steve McCaffery), L=A=N=G=U=A=G=E/Segue, New York,
>   NY, 1980
>   ***Tjanting***, The Figures, Berkeley, CA, 1981
>   ***Bart***, Potes & Poets Press, Hartford, CT, 1982
>   ***The Age of Huts***, Roof Books, New York, 1986
>   ***In the American Tree***, National Poetry Foundation, University of Maine,
>   Orono, ME, 1986
>   ***The New Sentence***, Roof, New York, NY, 1987
>   ***Leningrad*** (with Michael Davidson, Lyn Hejinian, and Barrett Watten),
>   Mercury House, San Francisco, CA, 1991

This book was made possible, in part, by a grant from the New York State
Council on the Arts and the National Endowment for the Arts.

ROOF BOOKS
are published by
The Segue Foundation
303 East 8th Street
New York, New York 10009

N/O

NON   OZ

Being two parts of *The Alphabet*

NON

For Jackson Mac Low

So then go back
                    to the old forms
          as if they were forms at all

wood frame
of a new structure, a theatre
soon to be covered by stucco
sort of a foam cement

                         or across the street the small
                         delicate elderly Korean lady
                         with her thick
                         and curiously deep red hair
                         squats in her garden
          so damp that frogs thrive
          coming up from the creek

          sun to my back
                    blanches the hillside
     each eucalyptus still as a candle
                    tho we feel the breeze

                         She rises
                         wearing green rubber gloves
                                   long stalks
                         of yellow-headed weeds
                         in hand

Continuity demands a margin
What is the import of detail?
How do we stake that claim?

          Here we fathom connection
     each word an accident of letters
               ink bleeding into the page

     the cage is open
     but the canary's dead

     Dylanologists who bet on the wrong man

Sam Donaldson shouts
over the copter's din
the prez he home
but nobody in

Little hill shrouded in rain
the way shingled houses streak when wet
or the concrete block apartments
with their bland identical drapes

women my own age
making the transition
away from youth

telling the barber
I part it on the right

fever crowds the brain
its thinking convulsive

porch lights on signal winter dusk

man in a three-piece suit
with a buttoned-down shirt
but the striped tie
hangs loose in two strands
holds his briefcase in his lap
open, a kind of desk

compulsive eye,
mottled world
old friend but an unfamiliar street
too brightly lit
sharpens the dark —
big glimmering headlamps
cars behind them not visible
float past

as the reader turns the page
you glimpse the shape of stanzas

What's the plot of this song?
Be sure to include the quotes

dim blue lights
    leave tunnel in shadow
          bright burst
      arrives the station

              one-legged woman
           swings on her crutches
        onto the escalator's
             first step
          shining black skin
              pulled tight
           and through her nose
                two gold loops

Imagine light
as a kind of firmament
this small metal lamp
a ground to write by
pen's stiff spine elongated
shadows to swallow letters
merely a shining pole
upon a wide black base standing
on an old walnut dresser
bulb's socket held aloft by a black clip
shade a cheerless plastic
from which hangs an insulated cord

           refrigerator's hum
        is joined by furnace

      the case is made of wicker
      and the top is arched
      shelves so deep
      that in front of the books
      stand small framed photos
      and a basket

try to write
without shoes on
tight grip of canvas
focus thought

setting the book down
I roll over and kiss you
bumping glasses
    up my nose

orange enamel kettle
atop white stove in kitchen
(harsh overhead light)
its wooden handle, tho treated,
has been blackened by flame

    small bowls within bigger ones
    is the right way to stack them

asleep beside me, you grind your teeth

two needlepoint doves in a circular frame

I hear the rhyme by accident
does not equal
accidental rhyme

    earlier
    your left hand gripped lightly
    the base of my cock
    so only the tip
    passed your lips

    sperm mixed with saliva
    spilled onto my belly
    you stirred it with your finger
    inside my navel

Brilliant postcard of Godzilla downtown

                    taking my hat off
                            is sometimes as dramatic
                                    as stepping outdoors

                as the play commences
                one begins to notice
                props on the table
                at the rear of the stage

                                            she wears her shirt untucked
                                            to elongate the torso

        in Beijing
                    Col. Sanders' name
                            translates into
                                    "Elder Head"

                the Hac Man with his flap down

                    Discharge planning

            in academic theory
                    the primary principle
            is defensibility

                                            from one letter
                                        generalize an alphabet

                    add civilization to weeds
                    yield flowers

                                            What're you doing, asks I
                                            Sucking bear, says she

                    eggwhite, eyes of the blind

        gulls' cries echo
        up from the valley floor

                              after the cold
                              the bus
                              hot as a sauna

bread truck's dolly
is in fact
 a stack of shelves

               silent radio electric kiosk

  the particular itself
  exemplifies the typical

here disjunction's visible

                         because spatially figured

        just for you

                    bright blue plastic tarp
                    atop the unfinished wood frame house
                    work stopped by the rain

   distinct patches
   back on the wing
   of the black-shouldered kite
   small otherwise white hawk
   high over the grassland
   flapping to hover

                    road barely visible
                    thru windows fogged in the rain

Ted's sonnets
mimic Jackson exactly

                              therefore here
                  little spasms of light

O parking lot
oh parking lot
I'd give my arm
to find a slot

shattered umbrella

bent

awkwardly as a broken bird

morning markets meaning maybe

old disposable
diapers
tied in knots
atop the black asphalt

almost blue
barely visible
smoke spews
from a red brick chimney

weird social movements

(*save the snails*)

my little chubbette

imagine Nobel laureate in chem
as political, as pathetic
as those in lit

homeboys in the rain eat brain

After three days solid
indoors
the shock
of the bus

I struggle to keep the shoulder bag from slipping

                galoshes
        that don't quite stretch
                        over old loafers

                                        thumb-size
                                hummingbird
                                still atop the branch tip
                                pips

        yellow light almost orange
        red stained furniture
        sun caught in the shades
        the gauzy curtains
        this door to the livingroom
        that to the hall

        gaudy rings on the cashier's fingers
        undercurrent of banter
        half-teasing, half-sexual
        between checkers & baggers
        I want my wares "double-plastic"

                                a beard to hide
                                the wide neck

                        rough edges
                        to fresh clipped nails
                        catch on the sweater

deliberate as the lack of path
                is the forward motion
        while the gull shakes and flaps
                        big teeth form a beautiful smile
        one man stands on a garage roof
                with a small bucket of hot tar
        here, closer, another man
                        pulls a blue collar
        up over his sweater
                sleeves bunched up to the elbows
        or a tall young man in bright yellow pancho

holding a day pack in one hand
grabs a seat
write what you see
but not to privilege sight

fog diminishes the horizon
the biosphere is shut
a man with dark hair on
the back of his hands
the curtains always drawn
on massage parlor windows
ears sting
in crisp air

green plexiglass awning over rear porch
on the highschool football field, the goal posts are rusting
an RV wrapped tight against the elements
woman with a mole at the corner of her mouth

"which section is this?"

"Oh, it's the mess"

I eat a banana
the way some men make war
to exercise my faculties
fully

said the regent
What does not change / is the difficulty
making change, coin vendor
"not in service at this time"

bag of salted
sunflower seeds
corner ripped open
beside the fat
paperback novel
atop one of a row of six
plastic seats
by the laundromat door

businesslike, an informality
that is almost intimate
yet impersonal as a hospital
rolling a cartful of wet underwear
to the wall of large, whirring dryers

> everyone's bundled
> even indoors
> but for the mailman
> in his short-sleeve shirt

> the sake of a story
> an autonomous thing

the whistling banker

random access remote

graffiti
on the walls
deep in subway tunnel

"I am attracted and repelled"
begins the review

> I am spatial memory
> he wears the kerchief
> pirate-style
> you raise your hand
> into which to cough

Balloon in the shape of a blimp
hangs from a long cord
although "hangs" is the wrong word
for the thick string nearly anchors it
over the brand new Mexican restaurant

> you think you're naked
> all dressed up in freckles

blanched light of haze preceding rain

                              pigeon struts
                              pecks at a cup
                              composed of styrofoam
                              containing coffee

            brittle rustle of the new
            plastic shopping bags

                        poultry is like a swan
            but with a (your pun here) —
                        railers and oos of the South Pacific
            for the most part extinct
              women who reread
            the Bible on the bus,
                              the way my knuckles
                                    foretell rain

Off the wall, Motherfucker!

is that how that went?

                        a new neighborhood
                        means a new idea

            avocets on the mudflats strut

        paltry is like a swine
        but with a diffidence,
        law of supply and DeMan

                              the folly of labor
                              on a Friday
                              seems particularly abundant

            that's not how you pronounce that

                  Budget Bob
                  offers a zircon pendant
                  Call Now

            (workers of the word unite)

a morning league for seniors
here at the Albany Bowl
already the air blue with smoke

a tiny Chinese couple
quite old, obviously in love
hand in hand with aluminum canes
almost identical deepset eyes

cranberries loom
in muffin's steaming flesh

two old guys in a pet shop
crowded, smelly, full of shadows
guinea pig in a cardboard box
and here on a rack a book on finches
those old color plates of the 1950s

you walk into the post office
and groan to see the line
tall stack of tax guides

a world here of children
means that time will pass

balloons tied to No Parking sign
hair stylist has a grand opening

I offer this sock
to the gods of the laundromat

then I wonder
about the number two

black tipped wings
one million snow geese
startled
thunder into the squawking sky

"Transit Shanties Firebombed"
page one head in the *Trib*
is not even mentioned in the *Chron*
marketplace of ideas

          cheap shot
          tipped at the rim
          drops in

     large dead boxer pup
     carcass unmangled, not even bruised
     still at the shoulder of the road

man on a bus
eating what appears to be
an uncooked hotdog
the way you would a carrot stick

          page fills
          like a sky with clouds

so tired
even on a Monday
some riders rest
their heads against the glass

     imagine space here
        as airy, fluid
   positions barely (and arbitrarily) fixed
            then instead as rigid
      etched

     pigeons coo on a crossbeam
     making me nervous —
     the narrative (implicit) slams shut

wad of gum
in the hair of a child
as an act of bullying

decades after
remains intense   —   tho I've forgotten
                                           just who they were
                                  wondering rather what drove them
                           what need to establish rank
                                           where elsewhere
                                  was power's absence
                                                        felt as need

    gull tilts its head back
    to cackle old gull-cackle
    atop a light pole in the mall lot
    glowing in the rain

                                  she twists
                           her head and
                           whole upper body
                                  to cast
                    long hair back over her shoulders
                                           and it takes my breath

    light pain behind each eye
    almost pushing, almost pleasure
    giddiness of too little sleep

                                  woman on the street
                                  to her companion whines
                                  "but I've *heard*
                                  of mutant turtles"

              Emma Freud,
                 Siggy's great grand
                daughter tho
                                  by her own
                    admission's
              never read word one
                    of his, stars
       on a British (I think) TV talk show
                    Pillow Talk
              on which the gimmick
       is that each interview is conducted

                    22

                    in bed,
          she and the celebrity both
                              wearing PJs

          young woman on a park bench in the brisk sun
          eyes shut, knees apart, and on each
          hand with the palm turned upward
          thumb and middle finger lightly touching
          international symbol for meditation

older woman here
face a virtual grid of wrinkles
thick white brows, eyes peering out

                    smokey morning light

          a woman's shoe, slipper-like
          twisted and bent
          abandoned at the busstop

                    the tops of the buses themselves
                    bear giant black numbers
                    intelligible to helicopters
                    lordly and isolate insects
                    kin to the dragonfly

          small blonde teenage girl
       skin so pale her freckles seem red
          blows huge pink gum bubble
                    which disappears
                    back into her mouth

"Do you do stocks?"
          Don't pollute
your commute   punctuation understood
                                   as a kind of battle
                                         necessary exactly
an old man   as words themselves fail
scribbling hurriedly
into a notebook on a bus

attack of the hard objects

owlish eyes
that sank deeper into gathering jowls
bracketed by cloud puffs of sideburns
the long cape, pale green suit, paisley tie
counting between lines by threes
or eating lunch at Panos'
sun glistening in the glass of white wine
really a pale yellow
I recall being surprised
alongside the stage that night at Glide
when someone (who? Linenthal?)
first brought Oppen up to be introduced
that you didn't already know him
(leaning his wiry, bent frame forward
to say "I want to talk to you
about your open vowels"

willingly we'll say
you were a petulant master

        chill air still

This morning the moon is chipped again
almost transparent in the predawn blue
high up over the eucalyptus

                          in panic
                    my heart racing
                            chest tight
                  not at the choices
              but at choice itself
                      which pair
                of cheap sunglasses?

        but the page you'll see
        is not this page
        (light red grid, lines
        too close together)

                    Ain't no toad
                    but a crow in the road

              man sees crow
              man writes about crow
              man eats crow

          clouds cast their shadows
          spotting the sea

Each letter conceals
The construction of its narrative
Beginning in fact with the teaser on the envelope,
Through the four-page letter, filled

With bullet-studded (·) lists, curious indents,
Subheads, key phrases underscored (possibly in color),
Leading up to the reply card, dear reader,
Upon which your favorite words (your name)
Are certain to appear
Alongside the word "YES"

              yes, she *is* the most desirable woman
              yes, I want *you* to lie on top of me so that I can kiss and suck
                            your breasts
              yes, let's rub pelvic bones until our pubic hair scratches
              or the way *my* tongue explores the inner curves of your ear,
                            sweet and waxy

so that she and you must be
and *are* the same person
even if you the reader is a boy
for what changes here, word to word
is what lurks behind the letter "I"
blur in the mirror, burr in the paw

                            he never recognized himself in photos
                            precisely because they *didn't*
                            reverse left and right

islands held clouds like a magnet

25

the plane itself is a shell
abandoned by bodies, filled by bodies
drifting in the currents of air

an alphabet of twelve letters
nearly half of them vowels
two of the consonants 'w' and 'r'
an alphabet without the letter 'r'

hang glider rider

        man on a surfboard with a paddle
        and his golden lab retriever

an old sugar mill
is being converted to a mall

        a tall wooden chair
        that to sit fully back in
        would leave your legs dangling
        so you find yourself invariably
        sitting on the edge

mynahs as common as sparrows

        double-decker dump truck

an itch under the eyelid

Instinctively
the damp mash of leaves, twigs,
soupy clay beginning
to give way beneath me, I
start to look for
strong roots to grab onto

        the descent beckons so slowly
        the hill itself collapsing
        I watch myself reaching
        fraction of a fraction of a second
        great nausea of adrenalin

hand locking onto the eucalyptus root
even time to wonder if
it will hold

a bowl of cool sour purple paste

housefinch with a nacho
hops to escape pigeon's rush

several juvenile
black-crowned night herons
share a pond by the airport
with the slender, pink-legged
black necked stilt

floodlights illumine
hotel garden

this page has been deliberately left blank

mongoose skitters across the lawn
like a big stretched-out squirrel

shit stained
black volcanic rock
pounded by the surf
is home
to the black noddy

abandoned jeep
is turned into a planter

zebra dove
much smaller than its mainland cousin
pale blue face

even the endemics
the "native" plants
arrived here
from elsewhere as seeds
in birds' stomachs

now that elsewhere's been lost

    the descent beckons
    trays returned to their "full upright locked position"
    landing gear down
    and infants start to cry
    their ears popping and
    them not knowing what that is

rewinding the tape
people walk backwards with confidence

        sox that slide
            bunching up
      in shoes' bottom

   big barf splash
      on the window of the bus
 upon closer inspection
    is the dried yolk of a thrown egg

        the children watch their parents
      watch the paintings
         noting carefully an attitude
      they'll learn as art

motorcycle's wheelie
cuts the still air

    cigarette's scar
    blisters leatherette seat

        the 't' in Tahiti

here becomes a 'k'
Kahiki, in Hawaiian
means "land of the fathers"
or did I make that up?

     semiotician = failed linguist
       oreos not arias

poet = failed second baseman
vireo video Vichy
the rice is white
fender bender parataxis
is there a fish in this text?
industrial occident

on sitcoms
the only prefix is 555-

puns invoke hidden rhymes

a military town
with few longterm locals

gaza stripper
Nonnie Sim

we took the fennel
thru the mountain

first a layer of bright canyon streaks
over which a second solid level
entirely in black
which is then cut into
to reveal the line

a word scratched out
leaves lovely shadow

you can hear a revision

land without roadkill

tort sure
not torch ear

in the utopia of language
so-called, why
are so many meanings homeless

you turn these to paragraphs later?
Tony Vaughan asks

                              Riding over Oahu
                              singing

Pineapple fields forever

        of the Olympic skater, says
        He's so impressed with his gold medal
        he's going to have it bronzed

    spider plant's web

                    taking off my hat
                    releasing weight and pressure
                    from brow

        contiguous: that's a word I seldom use

ambient hearing
like the way the driver
scans the road

        fluorescents hum in pairs

        yellow light of a shaded table lamp

                            shrimp feasts on caviar

            dog scratches behind locked door

                    beneath the paint
                    old sheet
                    of wallpaper starts of peel

        sudden burst
        several car horns at once
        means intersection's jammed

            between that and which

scar in the wall where
once a phone jack

           risers you can buy
           to alter table lamp's
           shade's relation

    syllables as a pulse
    larynx dilating or gripping shut

great crossbar of 'T'

        poem

             post-its as labels

              pages joined at top and bottom

        rust where once
        a paperclip held

                huge cup of lukewarm tea

leaves him bloated

          sun at the margin

                  water choking
                thru pipes in the wall

            multiples to go
            before I sleep

        naughty Liz
        not a less
        nor a list

      technique is a test of domination

                grand piano
             used as ironing board

Rock solid. Market wise.

The R-Effect

cursors
on the screen
are mean

dull fog
obliterates any background
the hill itself vague
as if hazily airbrushed

Hank calls himself
second-generation
victim of AIDS

I hadn't expected nature
to be so visibly a social construct
volcanic rocks
to which the whole world
has been imported

apple opal poplar dapple
sofa over ortho
grapples oval bother
opiate glover snaps
snits nick wicker wire
waffles after
further global sap wafer
waving gravy clover caps

pleonasts of the past amass

Tricks for modern scouts:
you can tell how long
a cigarette butt on the ground
by the bus bench
has been discarded
by how flattened it's become

     letting M&Ms
    melt in my mouth
    gradually, not biting in
     the smooth surface
    slowly turns coarse
    sugar coating
     about to give way

  flesh in the ear
  curiously dry and flaky

stools
like hard black large rocks

     little birds
    quarrelling in the tree

 in the dictionary
 the root of a given word
 is subordinated
 to its opening letter

I loves you
  Monkey-Mix

    odd the way a faucet juts
    from the side of a stucco wall
    overlooking nothing but a sidewalk
    with a pole to mark the bus stop

pigeons battling in the rafters

    old women
   heads wrapped in bandanas
   squint
    into the harsh wind

  string ties
  a boxed cake

long green trousers
beneath a white cotton skirt

suburban shopping district
      stores mostly closed
on a Sunday

      black exhaust spews
      from roaring bus

breathing
      through this phlegm

large number
red-orange
over which, superimposed
      smaller green letters
      san-serif
         lower case
            7-eleven

bulletin board
composed of stretched burlap

trope or trap

in Russia
      people sitting at a table
         over cheese, tea, bread
      chatting, no agenda
      is called "shuffling"

         bingo form
         each letter
         factored by fifteen

This is the way the word winds:
blind man's cane
forms a sort of sonar, scraping,
scratching a path across the dull walk
(grim faces await the train), birds

huddled in the pine branches, ache
in the knee; eyes
pressed against swollen sinuses.
Young girls in miniskirts
seem a generic sensuality
upon high school steps. I stop
to retie my shoes. A still
moment in early spring, half
in total bloom. Little metal whirr
of ball bearings in a skateboard.
The way a day pack
crunches a sport coat. The bay
half-visible through the dissolving fog.
Plate embedded in the red cement
is really a door, reads "water."
Train passes sandlot game of hardball,
pitcher in the midst of his wind-up,
leg cocked. Turning the newspaper's pages
in a confined space. Tension throbs
at base of neck. An odd day,
windy enough to demand a sweater,
hot enough to make you sweat.
It's not that the cap is tweed
but the broad green plaid
evokes stares (drinking orange juice
like a wino, tiny bottle
in a paper sack). Marks the margin
as if by magic. I search for scissors
to trim my beard. I heard
you were weird. Loading dock
for pick up, back
of department store. More ways
to pave patios where yards are fenced.
Hence nonsense follows. The truck itself
lifts and tilts the dumpster. Nuts,
caught between teeth,
increase pressure in skull. Hot spell's smog
smears the sky. Eye
of a pumpkin
rotting in the compost.

body heat
steams my own glasses, sweat
band of the hat soaked thru —
sweet salt taste

      the bridge rises
   out over the bay
        the eye sees
     dark towers
     holding the lanes aloft.

great zoo of my own species
        any subway stop

        ah hyper rush
       a spring day
          after hours of squinting
       at the amber screen

   first whine of the train
      as it rushes from the station

            first anniversary
          of the Grand Opening sign
          (bright yellow banner)
            of the Cozy
          Sheep Skin Seat Cover Shop

Once every six months
 like clockwork
I fuck over my root directory
   so that I can't boot from the C drive

fat wheels of a motor bike

            man in the row behind me
            does low, whistling bird calls

      Poets R
      satellite dish of the race

                              sun's glare blasts
                         thru the cracks

                    so thin
               in a down vest
                    the lollipop effect

     sits high
        in his wheel chair
     like a throne

                                   tho race itself
                                   be a fiction

          up close that tweed coat
        is a sequence of vertical bars
               filled with alternating
                    diagonal stripes

     there is no privilege in an end

                         hair without gel
                         looks like
                                   rhymes with
                              not so

               goes to Tahoe
               just to play the slots

     I turn my neck
     and the bones crack

                                   rough streak of stubble
                                   at beard's edge

          Proto-mallie: the flaneur.
          "The older I get the more
               floors I discover
          at Macys." Little red
          thermos looks like

fire extinguisher. Ants won't cross
trail of
petroleum jelly. Hat
with no bill, cubist
leather beret.
Sore on my tongue, smell
of dung. Voice's choices
sight's relight. In gaol
they make you surrender
your panty hose
to prevent suicide.
The crowd of protesters
approach, chanting
"out of the boutiques
and into the streets."
Seagull brushes
up against my cap.
Rude Work Ahead.
Velcro strap,
reusable cast.
Dog's name
is Cutty.
Eco-Brutalism, Deep
Semiology. Sturgeon
General. Boot failure!
Odd trim
of the ear's rim.
The neck seen
as a tube is
seen incorrectly.
Post-its peeking
from a three-ring binder.
Dog snarls
behind window of
locked Rabbit.
Morning's magic means
make my
daily bread. Ears
put head in
brackets. Hypervariables

in DNA show up
on screen like
bar code
on a cereal box.
Rushed writing.
One is to words
always an outsider,
tho they invade your head,
colonize dreams.
Neither an Aram
nor Omar be.
Picking your teeth versus
picking your nose. Voice
echoes up the lightwell.
Reading to discern liquids
from the bottoms of used cups.
Place mats
map the table.
De Man who shot
liberty: valence.
Blue sparks fly
in the dark tunnel
beneath the train's wheels.
The sound of an egg cracking
against the bowl's edge.
All sirens are narrative.
The brothers hover in the doorway
smokin' their crack.
Powdery sugar
atop apple pancake.
Now that we have computers
liquid paper is doomed.
Pair of grackles
attempt to mate
perched atop
Amtrak arrow logo
till the she-male
jumps into flight.
Water fountain's
cooling motor
hums on.

An odd john:
high urinals
and low basins
hard to tell apart.
Thimbalism. "JWs,"
he sniffed and sniffed he did,
"black Mormons." Yellow stone house
across the way, in which lives
Mrs. Florence Schneider
amid her treasures, rare china,
fine handspun cotton, a garden
of grape hyacinth — that odd
blue purple. Dump truck
pale blue filled with clay
atop which lays a shovel.
Black lores of the red cardinal.
Rounded shovel
is for cutting into
the earth, square ones
for piling it away.
Combination of
the swing and these
new reading glasses
quickly makes me seasick.
Back panel of greeting cards.

Just when you thought it was safe to read: Return to Planet of the Paragraphs. When this you see, justify right for me. Hills of the piedmont act as a track...along which the first long finger of oncoming fog is dragged. On the freeway cars cluster, herd instinct. The old man and the bicycle. Sun stuck in a web of cloud. Balconies unused in winter, swimming pool empty in the rain. Fractal tempo: cars rush past. Knowing just how long the "wait" light will blink before it turns to red. Mannish white haired woman echoes husband. Wide arc of bus as it turns. Categorize joggers by how they hold or wave their hands. Hard of darkness. Hanging from the ceiling of the Eyetalian restaurant was a huge plastic octopus. Theme park from hell. Where freckles join to form that small beautiful continent on the small of your back. Blue bursts of veins in the skin of the thigh. Walkers in the night take fright. Open, the briefcase in his lap forms a desk (train's roar echoes in the tunnel): he's using a calculator to balance his checkbook. Belt that missed one of the trouser's loops. Each sentence, dahling, is mahvelous. It's Monday and we're rushing to work — it's almost euphoric. Albino biker gal? Nah, that's just bleached out. Woman like that in spiked heels (briefcase is a Coach bag) running full tilt up the escalator to catch her train, trying to keep the *Wall Street Journal* from flying out of the crook of her arm. Each one bleach one. Nothing will tell you faster nor more accurately about the sexual allocation of labor in the field of architecture than women's restrooms in public buildings. Am I my brother's beeper? Yellow billed blackbird that I cannot find in the field guide. I turn over in bed and sense my sinuses drift and gradually resettle. Crisp lines of ironing shape the old man's blue jeans. The ice plant in bloom, red, yellow. Hegemony begins at home. Ragged looking plant, the artichoke. Hang gliders over the coast drift past the firing ranges at Fort Ord, almost motionless over the dunes (sand blows across the highway). Without a blink, the clerk pulls out a pair of scissors from under the counter and cuts the woman's credit card in two. Like a vomiter with the dry heaves. Suburban commercial street still empty at nine on a weekday morning. Wheels out of alignment. Abort, ignore, retry? Holding the pen virtually perpendicular to the page, thumb and fingers pinched near the point. Anklets over her stocking before she puts on her tennies. Readable? A cluttered desk is the spatial representation of over-commitment. Porch appears to have a roof, which in fact it does not. Old globe. Waiting for the others to choose their fortune cookies, so that I know that the one which remains contains my "fate." Bush hints at Deukmejian, all-Gemini ticket. Running up the steps, I blossom into a full sweat. Tables turned atop one another, cafe closed, man stands stationary alongside his mop. Anger augers altered ego. Duck into the dime store to buy an umbrella.

> words warm
> or warn
> where meaning wanes

> crouch to carve
> ink into pages

> moan as bus
> pulls free of station

                    Dan Rather
                 gives me a kiss

     "I'd like to buy a vowel"

                    hot sun
                    burgundy flowers

          balloons on a post
                    sign for a party
          drooping now, losing air

                              the page, the page
                              was all the rage
                    in the age of Olson
                    mock lung
          as the stumble of syllables
          plunge
             plunges
          space reduced
          to the details of representation

                    duet for grackle
                    and mourning dove

rake on a tractor
smooths the infield

                    break line at verb

          mob scene at station
          means the trains are late

                         simply shifting weight
                    bones 'pop' in the spine

driver returns to the empty bus
reaching in through the window
for the front door switch

ratty sweater
feels like home

so that linebreaks
are like parsing

when this you see
hold the bus for me

swabs of cloud
in the sunny sky

adults constitute secondary market
for boutique baby food "organic and wholesome"

problem of words
drifting across paper

hawk up
a wad of phlegm

in the park, by the playground
a little old lady, white haired
strums a banjo

symbolism of Uncle Tootie's house
where as a boy I mowed the lawn
overgrown now, gone to seed

a stack
o' flats   radio remote

pen's point feels cracked,
scrapes across the paper

Thick-browed albino
in an expensive suit

try to imagine
pigeons as nature

we just called
    that cowboy
        Hoppy

                        Samsonite briefcase
                 with red gym bag

    from gym to gum
    hum a hymn

                 deer body do breed

      boy with a perfect
          imitation
   of a pigeon coo

    it's not the tennies
    over her stockings
    in contrast
  to the tweed of her business suit
           but those white cotton socks

white haze
 of bright dawn
  through which
    a city rises
     pale silhouette
       while riders' heads
      tilt back
       the train asleep
         dawn commute
        or a man
          stares down
          into briefcase's cavern
         what "e"
           is ever silent
           to hold
              while in motion
           styrofoam cup
           so perfectly still
        large woman

                              pencil in teeth
                           crosswise forms
                      computer imitates bell
                      soft beep
                 door closing now
                      two women
                        in lace hats
                           speak German
                              blind woman's cane
                      folds up

What's hid (dawn grid): tendons scream in the knee
to ratchet the leg up a flight of stairs

                                        Lazuli bunting's
                                        copper chest
                                        beneath turquoise head
                                        tho brilliant, 's
                                        nothing
                                        paired with its song

           drainage pipe
                 channels creek
      to whose mouth, rusted
              hummingbirds come to bathe

                                             disavowal
                                             data verb

              I thought I'd lost
                this notebook till
              I picked up your gym bag

        lagoon at low tide
          rain's loosed anise air
                otter's head bobs up
            black-crowned night heron
        solitary, sits
                straw-billed curlew picks
        into damp, stony sand
                      white flecks

                   of an egrets' rookery
             high in the pine
                   feet in flight
             form a sort of rudder
             gull pleased to gulp a fish
                         tilts bill high
                   soft splash descends my grebe
                         the brush alive, crinkling
                   rabbits and lizards
                cormorant, rapid
                jets right over the water
                      still, grey — the enclosed sky
                asphalt road still wet with fog
                birders on the water's edge
             binoculars held high

eyes tire
        skull's socket
               is literal
             a fragile thing
                vase full of water
             on which a flower floats

                      for a week, for weeks
                      you seem about to cry

             egrets gobbles
             at their piping young

                                  the way a leaf
                      falling
                      spins in the air

I seek simple labor

                      up against the truck
                      harlequin duck

             anxiety determines the referent

Question:
"Where did I first see
a white-breasted nuthatch?"

Stifle impulse to answer
"In the mirror"

Siren on the freeway
            in opposite direction
blurts past

            Arm in a sling
      worn under
            short-sleeved shirt

                        train grinds
                              around curve
                        in tunnel

      pigeon drinking from a water dish

"The galleries of the new wing will be entered via a
'Grand Staircase,' leading the visitor to one large
and three intermediate sized exhibition spaces, each
broken by an interstitial space. From these spaces,
there will be windows — tantalizing views out to
the Pacific, which give the viewer a taste of the
'real' world before returning to the enclosed purity
of the galleries."

                        delicious
                        song
                        mocking
                        bird .

      brickwork as lattice

                        Advance button
                              on the tape deck

      default tab

in a proper linebreak the poet
comes to a complete and discernible stop

lamp holes punched
into auditorium ceiling

                        flame trees
                        of PBS

                        politics of X

            giant robot tortoise
            shell red and spotted
            like a ladybird's wings
            saunters forward

            pieces & coins
            rooms & corners

age has blurred
  the old man's tattoos
    chemistry is not prosody
        Dinnie dear
      the lake set deep
           atop the higher hills
             blue-green stain
           inkwell
      babies cry
           as the plane descends
      terrified
           not understanding
             pressure in the ears
                spoon scoops
                  seeds of the honeydew
                  my mind
                  instead of a bunion
                factories are not often
            many storeys tall
                turret vents atop
                spinning

he stops
to look at a book
on porn as addiction
springroll
and a sprig of cilantro
bound in lettuce
dipped
in the carrot vinaigrette
my page
instead of opinion
I strum
and the train rises
bicyclist's chain
worn about the neck
you yawn
and the silver flashes
"But I *AM*
Puss in Boots"
said Rae
towhees on the lawn at dawn
cafe over
bluff above the cove
beyond which
swimmers bob in the pale blue
between the shadows
that are reefs
reeves
works not
to read but
to read in
tie worn unlooped
hanging from buttoned-down collar
open at the neck
"pony nails," says Val
meaning the style of her hair
t-shirt under tank top
modesty on a hot day
four store fronts
topped with a row
of apartment gutted by fire
roof missing, interior walls

        surrounded now by a scaffold
    clouded whites
        of the blind man's eye
                under the feathered
                    leather cowboy hat
                            stone in shoe under arch of foot

End macro. To own a car is to own a carburetor. Black tie on a hot
day. The pout of a young girl. Canoe upturned atop a minivan. The
hard disk was not a disk at all, at least not in the strict sense, but a
pair of disks, shining polished iron oxide, four sides readable
beneath the needle's scan. Jai ROM. Utility substation. On the Read.
Shopping carts in a parkinglot by the bank. Drums in the dorm. Re
bait: rebate. The circle is warped. The dog mopes in the small yard.
In the distance somewhere, through the thick rustle of branches, a
wind chime gently traces a scale. Hefty sack of potting soil leans
against the house. Jay's call a trilled chatter. Thumb's ache after a
night of bowling. Arcs and curves in the bee's hovering flight.
Dwarf lemon. Wisps of fog so light you need your sunglasses just to
see them. Rose twists to find the sun. Sound of a softball against an
aluminum bat. Once the small airplane's engine passes, distant traf-
fic fills the air. The two flies are a dark green. Flesh at the elbows
revealed an age. Nudity is in fact more mysterious precisely for
what it fails to tell. I closed one eye to see the page. That letters
beget words is more violent than we've imagined. Towhee in tree
peeps at me. O brave new pen! Shadows at the arboretum. Sign on
the RV reads Snack Bar. Hard edge of a half moon. Crow amid the
blackbirds threatens scale. The benches in the sand under the trees
in the grand concourse. The curl of dead leaves. The courage of an
awkward, ugly work. The hero with a thousand feces. Realm not of
kings but of middle management. Slow belch bottled in the throat.
That thing in his pants with a twist-off cap. Fjordism. Rev. Moon's
son is "reborn" in the body of an African boy. The Sparts' line on
the Afghan invasion is "All Hail Red Army!" A town in which not
all cars are yellow. His idea of tennis thoroughly conditioned by
overhead highlight shots from the eleven o'clock news. Downhill
from the word Go. Lyn hegemony. White trim edges a dove's tail
(versus, say, patches on a mockingbird's wings) visible in flight. A
sentence bounded by the history of sentences steps forward.
Language is not my agent. Aphorisms attack. As plane as the nodes
on your face. Flower vendor's shaded stall. First green shoots on a

pruned tree. When this you feel, start to squeal. On the lawn under the tree in a bikini. Is a young woman without arms reading a book, bright orange highlight pen gripped between her toes. Mo, whose full name is Maureen, was as a child called Mimi. The sideways "2" shape of a curtain hook The well-wrought run. The word is all that is your face. Shit, boy, wipe yo' mouth, you got chocolate smeared on your beard like dingleberries on a hairy ass. Sparrow's shadow travels up stucco wall. Problem of drought etiquette: whether or not, at a friend's house, to flush. The Nortonsville dead are for the most part Welsh, recruited to the Black Diamond coal fields of California, suffocating for low grade ore in the 1870s, five towns no longer visible even in abandonment, houses moved elsewhere (to Antioch or Concord), hawk in a low glide over the dry hills, tombstones chipped under a grove of cypress, tho from down the hill, facing north through the valley, you can see the Sacramento River right at the point where the delta ends. The quality of mercy is not strange. Foggy, pronounced "fodgy" — the purpose of intimate nonsense, babytalk amid lovers, is to articulate a space apart. Your turn to have the car today. A form of otherwise vicious habit can become a pol and be named Bruce Babbit. Dull shadowless light of a clouded sky. Each thin braid of these corn rows individually dyed. Lone burst of hair beneath his lower lip can hardly be called a beard. A bird in the hand leaves a mess. From Gilbert and George to Gilbert and Gubar. The task of management is surveillance. Book bagged in polywrap = safe text. At dawn in the distance the compulsive mockingbird riffs trilling spirals. Bee's buzz as a mode of song: volume equals distance. Seamy ontics. Bright rug atop pale carpet. Parsley in a pot. Thin wire mesh of screen before fireplace. Ich bin ein Satz. The opposite field. Desperately seeking Godot. Well, I was hoping you were writing something about this delicious dinner I just cooked you. Digestion recollected in tranquility. Smoke spills from the holes of the barbecue's lid. Dents on my car hood from where crack dealers sit on it during the day time. How spell agapantha? Trimmed tree, as hard-edged as the patio it lines. Unheated pool on a cool day. Mao cap with a logo — this one reads "Tsing Tao." Young man carrying a bicycle up the flight of stairs. What does not charge is the will to charge. Marilyn Monroe had six toes on her left foot. A net sack for thistle seed, intended for finches, hangs empty, swinging in the soft breeze. Hum of a motorscooter's engine as it shifts down to climb the hill.

By the river one sees the homeless
nearly as visible
under Mitterand as Reagan

        infrastructure of the past is vast

     the beggar with the baboon
          tourists leaning
            to photograph its bulging
                bright red ass
    is at a distinct advantage

                bananas at a Parisian street market
                with labels that read Del Monte

   impossible to pop
pimple with just one hand

     barker at the Greek restaurant
          breaks plates in the doorway
    to get tourists' attention
    stereotype posed as tradition

A French woman without a cigarette
(complete this sentence)

          radishes in spiced yogurt

     a poet's home
     anywhere in the world
     visible to the eye

              vast fields of sunflowers
              and all the cows are white

       first there's Raworth's moustache
            world renowned
       then there's Raworth's hat

in a matter of days

my English decays
struggling with the translation, Francoise
leans forward at the crowded cafe table
                to ask "What
                is 'giving him head?'"

O crickets of Tarascon!

You speak
the most unintelligible
English I ever
heard, sez Ian to me

                Mynah
                in the cage in the cafe
                knows to whistle

        dogs
            wander amid the diners
                        without interest

                        to read aloud
                under the full moon
                    at a medieval chapel

        versus

                        to shout
                        facing
                        into the mistral

        once the Nazis governed here

                    "Les Dents de la Mer"
                    old familiar poster
                    in video store window

        the flap flap flap
        of loose sandals on the walk

                    brain cells of the past, alas

judge the nation
by the calmness of its dogs

        I love prejudice, she said

perch baked in foil
with butter, tomatoes, squash —
and caraway seeds!

        if only Eliot Weinberger
        had married Carl Andre

    How do you say "asshole" in Dutch?

        to understand
    that inherently you are political
        and that politics
            is poisoned

    From where comes power?

        that the middle of the alphabet
          should fall
              between 'm' and 'n'
      gives rise
             to a blank space

my mother in Switzerland who served oranges cold

      Bar du Siecle Glacier Le Mamba

          in Van Gogh's room

versus
Stella at the Pompidou
the perfect site

      as if by accident I have done in my life what I
      set out to do. dark fish form shadows in the
      stagnant water. the garden is a formal garden;

the sky too offers its crystalline structure. the pigeon is our national bird. but I am yet forty-two. the sun sets right in our eyes. on this corner, on August 22nd, 1944, women came into the streets to offer us wine, their lips and themselves, and the men did also. the tapestry dates from the third century: it is impossible to tell which bird is being referred to. the face of the clock is a roulette wheel. this cluster of blacks in the subway turn out to be students from the Ivory Coast, thoroughly bourgeois. people stand in the doorway of the tombs to get out of the rain. snail retreats into the pit of its shell, vain attempt to escape the stone's heat. beware when someone adorns you in basil. a frisbee sails over the wall of the castle.

modelism never sleeps

The world is all that's in your face. Napkins crumpled on the table at meal's end. Horse on a hill. Drill's friction: the smell of burning bone is exact. Apioectomy? Template of an invoice burned into the screen. In the yard of the house behind, the Eskimos' dog yaps up to the fence. Too thick taste of cola. Thick white enamel pain over these metal chairs lends them an air of plastic. Black butterfly, edged in yellow. We both wake to the sound of thunder, sitting up in bed to stare out the window as flashes illumine the shallow valley. I recycle the mosquito on my wrist into the next life. In his last voyage, my grandfather's great-grandfather commanded two ships, the Erebus and the Terror. Winding headphone cord about pocket radio. Two apples bend the slender branch. Fly appears to be "rubbing its hands together." Petals of this purple flower, withered on the deck. The unity effect, being phenomenological, is strictly imposed. Lead-soldered tin cans poisoned the crew: they abandoned their ships trapped in ice, proceeding to march in exactly the wrong direction. For Isotoner, I propose the following ad campaign: a series of videos based on old rock songs, e.g., *Gimme Some Gloving* and *All You Need Is Glove*. She paces platform, impatient. Stout puffed neck of the black pigeon. Gradually, over many days, ants devour the sparrow. Woman in the rear view mirror. Dawn frost beads the hood of

the car. Vietnamese boy's slender, feminine face, all eyelash and
cheekbone. Remove all that seems "characteristic" about your work
until the deeper features show through.

Blighted ovum

the black car idles
before the garage door starts
to yawn,
               radio inside it
causing windows on the entire block
to vibrate
that way glass hums
or I feel it in my teeth
plugged as they are into bone of jaw
until the vehicle enters
& is swallowed
by the basement
  of the green
ranch-style stucco house

               chestnut backed
          chickadee
          no larger than
               the hummingbird

shrill burst
of a jay's cackle

               transit routes generate
          patterns of access
               as natural

recombinant corn
taller than anyone
sunset orange with toxins

     bulb of a helmet
     atop motorscooter rider
     bright red

stiff-backed walk
of a tweedy old man
tho the light's against him
no traffic in sight

                               kid steps on a curb
                               as if walking a tightrope

                  Engage the page

                      we feel your freedom

           young woman in laundromat
                  reading, frowning into the book
                  Story of O

                    plastic notches
                         in the back
               of the one-size
                     fits all
                  baseball cap

        Virginia rail
         lives in the reeds
            of the weedy marsh,
          is larger than a phalarope

                    rowboat alone
                    on a small lake
                    windless day
                    boom box blasting

        Tilted bank of solar panels
        atop flat-roofed apartment complex

                       short stubby handlebars
                       signifies mountain bike

                sweatsuit as formal wear
                this must be California

cylinder of ink refill
is a nude pen

that grainy feel
of your shaved legs

folds of flesh
on the bald man's neck

Skyline of a small city:
the highrises are there
but not in such quantity
as to acquire a sense
of their collective shape.
That long last tone
at the end of
a Chinese sentence.
Painter's pants
immaculately pressed.
Oak trees
in the warehouse district.
Mack truck cab
rolling without a bed.
change gears
this high in the mountains.
In the dream the boat
sways in the high sea and
at the far end
is a giant sphere, the ball
rolling in the rough
weather
in your direction
so that you must choose
either to be crushed or to dive
into the impossible water.
Powdery filament tissue
of old spider web.
Floor mats on the sidewalk—
he's cleaning his car.
Yellowing jade

                    needs a larger pot.
            Clutch up on the bat
            to quicken the swing.
                                A film
                of the filming
                of a feature,
                            to serve
                as filler
                for late night
                TV. Therefore
            conjunctions stitch the seam.
            Gracefully disabled.
                                Thumbingbird.
                Unable with that hand
                    to close a fist
                consequent
                            to a medical experiment
            participated in as a student
                as easy way
            to earn money.
             Heavy
             pause
               on
        every
            word.
                Slaves of
         aviation.
                Wisp of dust
                    tumbleweeds
            across hardwood floor.
             Six-sided solid,
             the signified
            always
             faces the street.
        Poem with a shelf life
            of just eighteen months.
        Double beep of quarter hour.
                When suddenly
            that part in your hair
            widens like a grin.

                    59

Medical waste
  floats ashore
  of increasingly cluttered brain.
My friends,
  I am that man.
                    The flan
        is the body.
                Titles
    are often misleading,
    subtitles seldom are.
                        Checking
            out the driver
            in the next car
      through my rear view mirror
          at a stop light
                (one never sees
        the lower body),
  thin ebony man
    with a long white beard,
            tricolor rasta cap,
      high sharp cheekbones
  that cause the eyes to recede,
      I decide he's a gentle person.
  Rolls of roofing
            turned upright,
          black cylinders atop the gravel.
                        There comes a moment
                  whenever
              I read my poem when
                  it is apparent
              it is terrible
                  I'm a fraud,
        no one would ever
          choose to hear
          or to read this,
  but then this moment of panic passes.

In Gargoyle 32/33, Dan Beaver writes:
    Reading *Paradise* is like trying to put together a jig-saw
    puzzle of entirely square blocks. There is, no doubt, a prop-
    er way to construct the puzzle, but until the perfect solution

is stumbled upon, the player will be left confused and angry. *Paradise's* pieces are what the author calls "perfect Silliman sentences." Perhaps, but the paragraphs need a little work.

Paradise is too disjointed to work on any level. It is not a novel; there is no plot, no characters, no beginning, no middle, no end. There are, granted, recurring motifs, but they seem to be present only because the author's pen ran dry, and he filled it back up with the first old phrase that came to mind. Perhaps it is intended to be one long, rambling prose poem, with images splashed across the pages like a Jackson Pollock painting. If so, it is too long; the images do not remain consistently interesting to the reader through its length.

The sentences do not hang together and whatever logic there is behind the book remains hidden in the author's mind. The pastiche style that Silliman employs is mildly interesting for the first three or four pages, but during that time the reader is not given any indication of a sense of movement. If the reader stays around for all 63 pages, he will be just as confused at the end as he is at the beginning.

There are moments, however, of insight, when the sentences almost form a complete thought. For instance: "What is morning/ A cat. Fed. Curls up on a kitchen chair. Sedative sunlight. Gauzy room. All the books written to be read on the way to work." There are other moments when a single sentence stops the reader cold to consider the thought behind it. Perhaps this is enough and all that a writer can hope to accomplish. But there is too much that should be dispensed with. The key to the style of *Paradise* seems to be embodied in a sentence that falls near the end. "If I revised, this wouldn't be here." He is probably right.

moon transparent in the morning sky

antique camera shop's
alarm blurts
as the key turns in the lock

yellow ribbon
around the open pit
reads "caution"

sun's glare diffused
in the scratched plastic
of old bus window

      two scarves
      make a sling

          a stack of pink
        ceramic pipe sections
                 atop the flat bed truck

the way you carry
the bike upstairs
one-handed
      hoisted over your shoulder

      woman in high heels
      turns her foot
      to snuff out
      cigarette on the walk

                 tea leaves damp lamp
              at the bottom of the bag
                 on the saucer by
                    the cup

milky residue
in the soap dish

        post contemporary
      like a chopped Harley
        driven by an older woman

      the car pulls
        in front of the house
jays cackling high in the eucalyptus
motor running

        plastic laundry basket

              filled with books—
                     it's moving day

stucco stripped from the porch
for termite work

          Dodgers dish doggy do

         the topography of this beach
           is not the familiar
   gradual incline
                  smoothed over by high tides
          sand fleas thick
              over the rotting kelp
            cormorant's path
            low over the water
                but pocked
           anemone clenches
           to the finger's probe

  balloon of blister bursts

self-conscious, chasing
 the bus down a busy
   downtown street, his run
                   is a half
                     skip

Divide wire coat
hangers into
those with cardboard,
those without, those
wrapped in filmy white paper,
whether the hook is formed
by one metal strand or two, design
of the twist at the base
of the neck

        what I like most
        about the Albany Public Library
        is that it smells

the same as when I was six years old

Schizophrenoform

        It's not that
        there's a dead cat in the gutter but
        that it's been there all week

    snoodlenook

        Little moths under the porchlight,
        be with me now
        A dog in the distance
        barks compulsively
        Birds chirp
        to greet the early dusk

the landlady lives at the foot of the stairs
that run down the hill beside the house
so wooded you don't even notice them

          Dreamlike,
        the color TV
      thru the neighbor's gauze curtain

  ice crackles as it melts

    nibbling Cracker Jacks from the palm of my hand
    the little man in the blue suit salutes

the runner forgets to run,
so is easily forced at second

    as the earth pulls back
    dropping away from the rising jet
    one sees traffic
    recede into patterns
    individual cars the colors of candy
    slant featherwise
    amid the vast black field of parking

Song:
I said over and
over and
over again my friend
I really fear
that we're in the mirror
of production

Soft horizon — the clouds are nearly (but not entirely) unbroken,
level at the top, sun-whitened, but here and there: pockets, dimples,
canyons. Economy of detail is a value of distance. The way clouds
bunch, snagged by the mountains. Pen's tip is hidden by hand's
shadow. There are in fact two windows, one inside the other (it feels
like a thin plastic). Another jet no more than the sun's glare refract-
ed parallels our own path, but to the south. In a tight housing market,
exchange value overwhelms use value, as people purchase homes as
part of an explicit strategy of accumulation. Women on the telly tend
to wear red. In the dream, there's an ornate dresser with high legs,
its wood a polished blonde, beneath which a young man is hiding,
trapped, an enemy — how do I know it's an enemy — unable to
escape, for on the one side stands Barry and on the other myself and
I'm holding the fluid of a huge and heavy egg, shell gone but still
within a filmy translucent membrane, so large I can barely keep it
from spilling over though I'm using both hands, and I hurl it for-
wards as though I were a child and it a bowling ball far too large,
and the yolks bursts, yellow spreading over the hardwood floor, so
that the enemy, young and blonde — I don't think he's myself — has
no choice but to crawl through it before coming to confront us,
which he does, slowly standing as the rich yolk drips from his arms
and clothes. Next to me on the airplane is a woman with a long pair
of scissors, cutting coupons she's torn out of old papers, trimming
the edges with great exactness, placing them carefully into a box too
small to have held shoes which she's placed in the lap of her sleep-
ing husband, while I wonder about the wisdom of sharp objects in a
vehicle proceeding at 600 mph. From where the cars exit the park.
Emma says to her father, "You're the head of words." A sushi bar
with a maitre d' in a black leather tux. "Photography is not permit-
ted," says the sign at the entrance to the Nicholas Nixon exhibit
(each sequence in the series of PWAs concludes with a note as to the
date of death of the subject). Anselm Kiefer's winged palette: only
once in a thousand years does an artist come along who can lead the

German people. At a station of the IRT: an apparition of Jack
Lemmon crossing the street. In actuality this means a watery yogurt
whereas I prefer mine thick as custard. What's better than a new
pen? Green-framed dormers of the Dakota. He speaks of the instru-
mental function of poets in his homeland, Ghana, by which he
means funerals, births, weddings. The pigeon picks at the muffin,
tossing it in the air, then abandons it to the next in line. He sits cross-
legged on the tile circle, directly above its lone word, "Imagine,"
while his mother squints to focus her camera. I stop at the produce
market just to buy a lone banana. Others come up to the tile circle,
then step back, careful not to touch the sacramental spot. Oh field of
squirrels and brazen sparrows. Leaves gather on the red brick steps:
four pairs of rectangles "woven" into a square of eight. Willard
Rouse's neo-deco dildo dominates the sky. Pensive people. A police
officer with a noticeable limp ambles asymmetrically through the
marble lobby of 30th Street Station: flipping sound of Amtrak desti-
nation sign. Echo of the subway corridor enhances the beggar's song
("There is a rose that grows in Spanish Harlem"), vowels stretched
over the tiny portable organ's chords, while in the distance, from
another corridor, I hear the lilt of Peruvian flutes. They're sitting
side by side on that bench, but are they sitting together? "I quit the
theater to go into politics because I was tired of dealing with huge
egos." An old man with cotton plugs in his nostrils and ears. The
thick lower lip protrudes over the firm jaw, softened by the spread-
ing neck, the hair above still thick and wavy, tho graying, beneath
which shoot the stems of tortoise-shell reading glasses set upon the
soft pyramid of nose, long-lobed ears set close to the skull, great
thick pale brows balanced by the curiously thin upper lip.
Correction: an article on Nov. 1 about Imelda Marcos' appearance at
an arraignment hearing in Manhattan misstated her shoe size in
alluding to her reputation for extravagance — the size is 8 and one-
half. A Mali ladder on a metal base makes for a narrow, vertical
sculpture, and is priced at ten grand. Teardrop pear. The loft quivers,
meaning a train in the subway is rushing past. In the middle dis-
tance, the Chrysler Building's tower blurs: it's begun to rain uptown.
Pear's flesh so hard that my gums bleed. On the cover it reads North
Point Press * San Francisco (but it's not San Francisco) and on the
press release North Point Press, Berkeley (but it's not Berkeley), the
glossy author's photo slipping to the table (collar open to reveal the
hair on his chest): it's the small house next to the laundromat,
Albany, CA. On the back slope of the cemetery, the stones are small-

er, dark and twisted. Detention Windows, says the fading factory sign, For All Your Locked Facility Needs. Red painted tips of two-by-fours, blonde boards stacked high, lumber yard in the rain. I plug one ear with a finger as I shout into a phone at Penn Station, talking to my wife whom I've not seen for a week, asking if she still has all those freckles. Old ties lie by the side of the tracks, black chips. Hello there, Zed heads. Odd intimacy to see women asleep in their seats as I amble back to the dining car (how many are simultaneously wearing headphones?). Autowrecking yard at the edge of the river (which came first?). *Concurrence*, in French, means *competition*. What is the name of this harbor? A field of abandoned buses. Thinking hard for all of us, I honked, and the deer bounded into the wooded dark. Great brick cities of the east. Charlemagne Palestine slaps you in the face, softly, but aggressive enough to mock your commitment to pacifism (Bruce turns to Anne and says "Deck 'im"). Having fallen behind, it feels that we are rushing now to the next station, the next letter, the dawn hidden in the trees like so many raisins amid branflakes, my heart pounding, skin aflame with blood flushing through. Gulls in the sand at shore's end, sun glimmering in the mottled water. Thick web of leafless branches, little ponds of dark water — abrupt hamlet of white wood-framed homes. Interlocking design of townhouse condos. And then went down on her lips, set tongue to tip, forth in the twisting night. Behind the house, a cluster of rusting trucks. Bob is a dog, in fact a bouvier: at this rate of growth, in one year he'll be the world. The papadum is crisp. Three women discuss problems of their cordless phones. The conductor slumps into a chair in the cafe car. Poem waiting versus poem forwarding. Meaning is forever homeless. Jose Canseco twitches his neck. The hang time of telling. Evening is as morning does. Surgeons of the future, suture. *Mais langue n'est pas langage.* Toweling Trades Training Center. Old jet trails diffusing into pencil-thin clouds, beyond which a translucent half moon is already visible in the noon sky, a blue so pale it tends toward yellow at the horizon. Theory of chutney: sweet cuts hot even better than water. Pylons where once bridge stood. Blackbirds over dry fields. You pull your legs up so as to slouch down in the confined space of the train seat. The city is fast approaching. She offers you a slice of pie, but calls it "apple cake." We pass these cars so rapidly they appear to be sliding backwards. Verb tense and sentence length are all you need of narrative. The fly hovers high over the infield. In the distance, clouds break the sun into a brilliant orange-red. I can see this in your eyes.

OZ

For Fred Glass & Maureen Katz

Forms farm storm's harm.

Imagine a language that worked.

ironic,
euphoric

Medicine is not narrative. Blue trashed sky. Firemen on ladders into the
smoking night.

Phlegm fuels cough. Yellow triangle: abstract banana. Money is the aura of
art. Consonant etched into vowel. Mexican comic (comment).

Let us go then, I & I,
outward. For
get focus, for
giveness. Enclosed please find
dropcloth wainscot Orion
simmering middle management
Dobermans at racquetball
fine tooth comb

Hum job. Modernism hopes for a lawn. It's hat time. Symmetry in let-
tuce's system marked by types. Breadstick wedged in the dip. Waiting for
Conan. Ponytail in hardhat sells tobacco. Peripherals for my new stanza.
Powder detergent. Team meeting. Break-in-the-clouds symbolism. Warrior
earwig along garden walk. Sun's warmth on your forehead is different from
being smart.

That's mean. That's meaning. Under glass at the deli pigsfeet sit in a pan
of pink juices. Laces knotted together, red tennies hang from a power line.
Blue bandanna about the pit bull's neck. Analog sky. They seem so lost in
thought on the bus on their way to work, still yawning. Chinese shoes of
black cotton. White shades appear blue behind tinted glass. Once they pay
the driver, their eyes scan the tubelike bus rapidly, searching for a safe
seat. Prospect identification. Package of the Year. Ultrasound poetics.
Sound of buzzsaw and rooster. Squish of tires over wet streets. Cloud-fil-
tered sun mutes colors amid valley houses. Words scratched out, arrows to
new syntax. These vowels my eyes. Lack of trees in all this snow signifies

lake Smoke still in the air from a wood fire. Alarm in a locked auto carries through the night.

Theme is trees
them is "-atic"
park verbs auto
versus forest havoc
foot foot foot
Columbia mall moped
on a motto
poetic cheap trick
macho but wounded
stage whisper persona
the too-clean garden
short fat word
perfect for tenure
is the night
constellations an order
connect the dots
to organize sight

Change in fund balance
atomic table water table
your haircut's too political
bison crossing cavern wall
kung fu lunch pail
view of the harbor
additive, but not personal
sometimes a great lotion
pick a dirty penny
soft sound savage sense
fosters apparent cohesion, a
ruse is a ruse
is not the next
allusion, lines are bent
spines against the margin
spin a hardening version
jetlike to the heart

Exit to system. Striped tie divides a great expanse. Pressure sensitive, duplicates purged. Cat sleeps atop car roof. Through a window I see the pocked bottom of an iron atop a tape reflect the red evening sun.

Many sirens: bad news. Such a small old man to be a bank guard. A brown van. Simple syntax yanked them into plot. A bad thing.

Over the fencetop the tip of a bush suggests a richer foliation. Dull scrim of cloud yields colorless day. I let the first bus pass, hoping the next would be less crowded. Each sentence resolves a battle. A title, not a caption.

Pastel acrylic of a flowerpot decorates gallery wall. Chipped cup. Web of powerlines segments sky. Nouns accumulate on the floor of the car. Article is found benign.

At the wheel of the truck I see a nun. Design of the lid of a styrofoam cup. Intense first taste of spring. The question in Hoagy's case is not which side pulled the trigger. An inalienable right to choose nylon.

The asymmetry of your make-up is not intended. Giant tear on cheek of clown. The margin in the mark-up. Big blue truck of the Starvation Army. A mind is a terrible thing to face.

Seven come eleven. These women share a moment, watching their children at the playground. An older lady in sensible shoes. The billboard alters the scale of houses nearby. Flashing yellow lights.

A glass parrot hung in the window. The function of the tiger cub in Michael Jackson's *Thriller*. Blue shading surrounds an almond eye. Small girl skips along. Please pay amount due.

A burning in the bowels. With the window open, the curtains flapped in the breeze. The cord from her headphones led into her purse. A sentence with four strong beats. On the windshield of the car was a sign: For Sale.

I accepted the assignment at scale. Behind the high fence was a tiny boxlike house. This is not syntax. Her red hair glistened copper in the sun. Autos parked on an empty residential street present an image of form.

Caution, frequent stops. The paper has a business section, but never one for labor. The library rebinds its paperbacks. Plaster madonna framed in the window. The half light of the violets.

Ankles away. Parallel function of the I Ching and DSM III. As we age our features turn into caricature. Her stocking reduced the bruise to a shadow. Humor in uniform. Placement is not random. The hacking coo of a pigeon in the lightwell. Brown-white lumps of old snow in the gutter. The rigor of the big trucks. The Eastern Shuttle. Carrying the proofs of Blackburn's Collected downtown on the IRT. Little cubes of frozen carrots. I recall the taste of the tip of your tongue. Under the overpass a group of men huddled around the burning trashcan, their only light its deep orange flame. As Richard Nixon said, "I am not a language poet." Russ & Daughters kosher deli: amber bowl of salmon caviar. Hip-hop, the crews are breaking. We meet by chance at Saint Marks Books and the politeness is awkward. He hands me some poems "for feedback." California boy that I am, the last thing I expected in New York was the stately sound of hoofbeats in the night. The person at the end of the sentence. The radiator hisses and bangs throughout the night. Elbows in, palms upward, spin on heel and toe. Breakers' theory of the shoelace. I'm not responsible for every Jew in New York. I really love you. Words wall emotion in, the verse of a conduit. Not a one of my friends there has a garden, a houseplant or a pet. The mall is a cluster of buildings in the center of a sea of parking. How thin the gravestones seem. Tennis courts empty in the winter. These clouds feel like solid objects suspended from the sky. Memoirs of the Philly Zoo. The "blonde" in the photo hugging Michael Jackson turns out to be Charlie's mother. I dream that I'm trapped in a drug bust with Connie Francis. The large boned dancer stoops. Tricep dip. A thick dal. I can never travel without being aware of the choices I've made. I watched myself telling her that, even under other circumstances, I didn't think we had a future together, feeling distant, nauseous, the disaster coming true, myself to blame. Kansas City but a patch of lights beneath the night sky. Power padded, value added. On the Sufi track. An old news and cigarette stand, single narrow storefront corridor, but they call it Gem Spa. Velcro flaps on the old woman's shoes. Duncan's dialysis. Seniors that wear greatcoats on the hottest of days. Old poster on a phone pole, words missing. Proud of his cute Jeep. Jogging in dawn heat, the soft smells of spring trigger the taste of glue from my Davy Crockett stamp book 27 years before. Ellen Zweig, dyed blonde, her hand on the shoulder of Armand Schwerner. Seeing him dressed in coveralls, paint in his hair, I guessed at his work. memory is not rational. Cuticles of pleasure. Oppen in a rest home. Everyone on the bus is wearing headphones. Spirit disinvents number: lint balls blow across the plane. The new reality is the old one (say it with a smile). The lizard of odds gambles with crisis punctuation (nouns rowdy with substitute clause). Sit down, small bear. Art bean. The files are restless: fluorescent bulb flickers on. Write me a ticket. Ears as hooks from which to hang glasses (batch it): your bra unsnaps in front. Port in the haze silhouette — the East Bay is missing. more elaborate floral arrangements index middle life (no strain, no pain, no gain), airbrushed nudes tacked to shipping clerk's wall: the presidency is just a reflection. Later she will replace that thumb in her mouth with somebody's penis: you probably think this song is about you. An illusion of logic gets you to the job, an architect's drawings by free association, lead deposits in a phone bank, all of religion compressed in a condom, mathematical representation of chaos: the exogamy of want-ads perceived as a face. Pregnancy is the mother of prevention. The ink fades to a monument, visible limp of denotation, flock of adjectives pecking at garbage in a playground. Snort clouds: a black girl shouts, "You walk like a faggot," one size fits all. Stop me before I write again. She visits him in the convalescent home, a kind of pre-widowhood. The dark lashes clash against the light, freckled cheek. Details of a universe generalize for consumption, a Sunday stroll through the industrial district (the earring caught on her headphones): the overall's straps pretest gravity. Response device: the dependent clause is not benign (rose's thorn but a form of callous), the circuitry is blissed, an old math abstracts fingers (Trigger stamps out a haiku). Old bottles of beer and gin gathered at the bottom of the phonebooth. Her headphones leaked a drumbeat. The head is on duty (fire), a nervous attachment to hinges (sulfuric), self-confident machine strolling lazily through a field of tall corn, butterflies of all nations, dictionary's illustration of the range of flags (coffee beans in decorator colors): I spy. An astronaut in the bath is worth two on the hood (direct communication), transcendental medication (ears that rhyme never prime), violators towed. Dear Sequence, tar in a ditch (the windowsill is my garden). They call this abstraction person. Rubber stamps made to order, utility substation, bound frond (deliveries made in rear), nearer my Fifth Street to thee. Paper tigger. A sentence is defined as it's defied. Ooze orders snooze. The dream of fact is tuned to a waltz barely sublimated to the silence of this thick forest where light itself is felt as sound. Against this embroidered scrim men are cutting into the asphalt of emotions with a jackhammer. Literature's vertical hold, a belief in the ten's place has begun to flip.

An image of morning in the window
no more than light caught on the fuzzed
flesh of the violet flashes
a memory encoded as odor, cooked
carrots, of a more spectacular kitchen
which is only your grandmother extended
beyond her private language, the weeping
at the sink made song, the erosion
of particulars that renders an old nook
into a fond altar, splinters of its rough grain
more distinct than anyone who ever lived here
which of course we never did.

White against white, birch in the winter forest
photograph in the pharmacy's free calendar
brings January to a wall in May
in a small room, the torn shades
still capable of shutting light
into shadow, the small hands
of the old man rolling tobacco
into cigars in this storefront
halflight are as brown as the
leaves, an image without music
in the hot spring air where now
there stands a parking lot.

Anger as action yields
the danger that factions
wielding power deformed
for the sake of a story
mourned for its climax
as a form of
gloryhole titillation
can only create
the sensations of song,
the beat of the drum,
the round of fiddles
playing rock.

Continuity as a process
with which I am not
familiar (here I
transfer buses), who
speaks, who listens, how
is one, any
one, to speak, to
keep to the same
I without blinking
(pad pun, Mr Old
Song), the stutterer
thinks to sing.

False start, true start, who
hardly harps on a theme

treads the stream's rocky
crossing (stone hinge), bones
impinged on by muscle
stretch: teach verse
in the face of adversity
(get a job), unrehearsed
the hand's search
is its own dance,
my lance spilling ink
in the place of blood.

Ceramic dog, head tilted,
seeks words not heard of
from an invisible master
not heard of, who forms
a model of the not seen
shadowy as static
across the sands of Africa
unfaithful in translation
as any garden image
of a young man, sad,
short hair disheveled,
so loved by Verlaine.

Tea cups in the dream as big
as hot tubs twirl and
dance, we in them (cream
of poets) in our own pants
with the cuffs rolled, cough
to laugh at some
broth of old poems, wilted
profs stirring the roots up
with a spoon so much
smaller at my nostril,
counter-intuitive, like
your simile's big grin.

Rhetor and phlegm, this sham
discourse trims the reader's
excuses, you are not
not permitted, unfit, to respond

nor is this your asylum, this
upper westside wall of words,
syntax my mortar, painted
nouns, a circus
for the faint world, hurry
up please it's time
the echoes of your own war
were heard in the poem.

Pastel, pretty as a needlepoint
seascape, an image forms
which is its own meaning
into which we pour
your ambitions, my regrets,
the shady, busy world
of office afternoons, radio
of the freeway commute, gravy
mix on potato flakes
mashed and scooped into a bloated

wobbling message, wrapped tight
for ease of consumption.

The mind lurches (a ball
of string as large as
the Farallons) forward —
that is, movement itself
creates the illusion
of time (do not
disturb), occupants
as we are to this
perspective, the sky
(blue) joins the sea
(green) off in a distance
that is our own.

MBWA: shoot between
heartbeats, one's eyes
register concentration, the mouth
intensities like the scale of
a thermometer, orange against black

the butterfly's scheme
is its own meaning (beetle's shell),
skull in the museum
with a stupid grin, clarity
(caffeine in the nervous system,
sun on the garden's clover)
is strictly physiological.

When in doubt sit down
is zen's way out, thin sway
of body's logic, laughter's
just steam from an engine
heating, plums rotting
in damp soil, oil siphoned
from a veined earth,
one world I don't understand
but for being (not Bronk's
grim facade nor Ashbery's
cynical lime twist) a hummingbird,
a hummingbird totally out of place.

The symbolist is unable to see the forest for his parents. O tree of life
so full of strife, this knife is to carve initials. Slabs of sheetrock by a pink
roll of insulation (we are building the alphabet, a pyramid in the desert, a
campsite for the caravan, feeding the ostriches, the tiger, bonfires on a dry
night). My folks, who are Bengali, were teaching in Uganda when the
Second World War broke out. The tunnel is really a tube laid across the
bottom of the bay. You hold your arms straight up, waiting for me to lift
the blouse off. He said "I sold the novel," verb telling all. The eye, orange-
brown, rolled across the floor. Sweetbreads in a light sauce. Spray paint
over the marxist-leninist graffiti yields an inadvertent abstraction. If I write
more slowly now, it's because I've already said too much. Jerk pulls neck,
wins award. Garden party wedding reception. A low fog blurs the ink, each
word a stain. A summer in six sentences, ten. market segment. Front yard
gone to weeds, the stairs to the blue house lean. Plastic case in which to
keep her glasses. Life is detail (steep slope). A man sits on the steps,
waiting for a bus. (All that aside!) Fog this thick gives one the sense of
forever being indoors. Boarding the bus, she tucks half a donut in her purse.
Gary Hart bumperstickers fade to nostalgia. Page numbers date from 1499
(even they have a history, a politics). The dew sits lightly on the short
grass, not sinking in. A small front yard, fenced in, full of giant sunflowers

The stores and bars quiet at dawn. The first bus with its few passengers. My penis slips in easily and you pull your shirt off. Upstairs the neighbors are running the shower. The kitchen faucet with its slow, two-beat drip. Ice in the O.J. Romanticism dissolves the poet's marrow (the cells, the selves, reduplicating wildly out of control). The fern on the porch pleased to be getting more water. Jack-off clubs have come into fashion (shoes required). On a hot day the crazies still wear eight layers of clothes. Scratched and dirty, the bus windows dull the brilliance of the sun, glimmering on the boat-crowded bay. Blue pen, black pen. Trying to tell Rich Little from Little Richard. He steps on the glass to complete the ritual (it's wrapped in a napkin provided by the hotel). The dj coos into the microphone. Below, people are playing tennis or splashing about in the intense blue of the pool. The bridge forms a mark, familiar upon the horizon. Your sister in the next room, we fuck slowly, quietly, seeking silence in each orgasm. Andrei Codrescu is his own critique. The old loom sits atop a foot locker. On the windowsill the ceramic elephant in enmeshed in cobwebs, a figure of strength trapped in nets. Beginning the bench press (90 lb. weight), I felt my spine "crack," popping into alignment on the first lift. I shut my eyes and pay attention to my breathing. Refrigerator with no door is used as a bookshelf. We take turns in our movements (sex is a sharing). Imagine two men shopping for food as a thing to do together. Nothing is so reminiscent of childhood as a hot day. Your first lover is now an electrician. An irrational fear of personal vulnerability extends to a national scale and combines with breezy arrogance in the smile of the President. "America's movie... *Red Dawn*." Two sisters shout recipe details over the music of Cindy Lauper. On the toothpick, in this sequence, were a slice of red pepper, a scallop, a slice of white onion, a shrimp, and a slice of green pepper. One lives through detail. Wash, pronounced warsh. They listen to Boy George and speak in Tagalog. He sleeps on a beach blanket in a fetal position. On trash day, the Chinese woman from the next block goes house to house, inspecting the garbage, gathering tin cans in a large string net. Things people think to put on their front porch. The plural forms an abstraction. Trousers of golf culture. A generation of humanities professors turn into administrators in order to save their jobs. Fists half-clenched as he walks down the street. The carpenter is writing his dissertation on Thoreau. Little girl skipping to catch the bus. Hello, my name is Mitchell Omerberg and I'm calling tonight from Supervisor Harry Britt's re-election campaign committee. Last week we mailed you a flyer describing Harry's record with a form to fill out if you wish to obtain an absentee ballot and vote by mail. Have you received this yet? List composed of voters who've failed to vote in two of the last four major elections living in buildings of four or more units in liberal neighborhoods, purged of Republicans, landowners and those with no listed telephone for follow-up. In the dream the tattooed woman pulls her head back at the moment of the man's orgasm, sperm splashing on the tip of her nose. Same day service. In breakdancing, this move is called Furious Fish. Crows and rooster marking dawn. In the country the sporadic sounds of traffic comfort. These old hiking boots, never broken in. From the board room on the 51st floor of the Bank of America World Headquarters the entire Bay Area appears in a new scale, Bernal Heights a mere ripple in the topography, a chessboard on which individual lives, consequences, become infinitesimal (directly below, a hole in the ground where once stood the International Hotel). Here, concealed, lie two competing fictions: (1) that the boardroom, facing north, holds no view of Bernal Heights; (2) that, by the power of sheer height, lives might be abstracted, their contents banished. Saying makes it so...said the exit poll. Voices in the mosswood. Subtle greens, yellow-greens (the red of poison oak). "How can you write of a bank in the wilderness?" Ah, but that is the wilderness. Gartersnake slithers into the weeds. Horse shoe prints in the mud. She watches pelicans through field glasses from a cliff at coast's edge. This ocean, land at its margins, unyielding text. Where the sun reflects off of the water, the waves are the dark marks. I smell wood smoke. Champagne mimosa. The wild bay leaf. Fresh, the large cowpies are dark, almost black at the crust, a rich, moist green in the middle. Below, a line of reeds wanders through the dry grass of the valley, marking the trail of a brook. In the split-interest trust, the needs of the income beneficiary often conflict with those of the remainderman. Sunflowers growing atop a garage. Strolling into the office 45 minutes late. Turkey vultures circle over the valley. As, at the tip of my tongue, you come, your thighs tighten their grip on my head, your own hips rocking until now they begin to shake. Sliced apple. Bread crumbs and garlic atop the pan-fried oysters. Digging seeds from the watermelon with a spoon. Another Paradigm for Peace. First cold day of autumn, furnace on, the smell of dust burning. Orange plastic cones mark wet paint at a crosswalk. Fluorescent yellow of fastfood mustard. Call Barry. The busdriver's hairpiece. The theosophist's Yamaha (is not a piano). Typed so as to indicate scoring. The page of the manuscript (a vacant lot) is not that of the published text (Wrigley Field). The line drives to the margin. Preparing to write, I touch my cap, hitch up my pants and reach for the bag of resin. Shake off that metaphor. Language parrots the world (with as much understanding). A bench by the window in the study, overlooking the valley's vineyards, a low fog. A flock of small birds descend on one tree. Oz' odds: language was the wizard (not a wall of silence, but a well). Hard rock futon. The wind chimes are still. Footsteps on the stairs, first voices. The hour the most empty, the fullest. At first, pipes in the wall cough and rattle, but now there's a steady shush. By the little orange berry bush Tom (not that Tom) is shading his eyes from the sun's glare on the valley fog. Ten sentences a day does make. My nostrils, tho clear, feel caked with the cold. I feel the pressure points between this chair and these bones. Terrible blue sky. Twenty-two pilgrims walking along a country road. Large, moss-covered boulders. Bluebird as big as a kitten. The discussion heating up, one voice rhythmically insisting, louder than the others, "that's right, that's right." A woman's laughter. Woolworth's, that great trash cornucopia. Black cat sticks its nose into a cup of coffee. Old brick ranch house with a red shingle roof. Buzz of the dragon fly. The heat of the sun on my face versus the breeze in the hair on my arms. The tree's reflection versus the tree's shadow on the surface of the pool. Smell of wood smoke. One can tell by the sound alone that that small plane in the sky is turning, changing course, tracing and retracing the air over the valley. Bird glides into the tree. High up in its branches, one hears the rustling of lives. Thin clouds that appear streaked against the roof of the sky. I draw words, these letters as strange as any, listening to a bird's wings flutter in passing. Footsteps over gravel. The valley layered, its more distant ripples half-misted silhouettes, the vineyards red-brown. Cows moo. Like a lawn sprinkler, a fertilizing machine shoots long green jets out over the field. Out there, the small towns are visible only as lights glistening in the night. At dawn, the one distinct cloud is obviously the trail of a jet, long since passed. Birds in the pine tree chuckle. The tiny lawn "windmill" in the shape of a sunflower begins to spin. Weeks later I'm riding the bus with a new pen (it rains). Glaze of moisture atop the umbrella's surface. This sky is several shades of gray. Baby Fae is dead. Steam spews from behind the old hospital. On days like this I bus into work with no sense of hurry. A young Latino with a spiral snake tattoo is reading Judith Rossner's *August*. Middle-aged Third World man, quiet, works as a rent-a-cop (nothing to do in the bank lobby but stand around). House raised on stilts, awaiting a new foundation. Muscles bulging out of an alligator sport-shirt. I smell hot tar. Differing rhythms of people as they walk. Fists clenched, he runs for the bus. The rocker in the attic small enough for a two year old. One sentence for every reader. Two coils glowing behind a grid of bars, the heater hums. The chamberpot was a plastic bucket. Old farmhouses form a small town, alongside which sits the new mall. The crib in one corner is filled with books. My dear one loves her sleep (I sit and write by the dull light of a grey dawn). That, as it happened, was the central term in their language, gray, the sole word permitted alternate spellings, around which the vast field of other, proper versions, each of them arbitrary, grew. The cup sat atop the glass table, the tea within steaming. It was December and newborn lambs stumbled through the fields. The bar of soap was new, its features perfectly etched. The offshore rocks break the incoming wave. A golden rural schoolhouse where, once, Hitchcock filmed *The Birds*. Sun-dried tomatoes. White wicker couch. I can't find my hat. Thermos of chamomile. Web of wires over an intersection (how we break up the sky). Tiny American flag on the fire engine's cab. Silhouette of a 727, rising slowly headed north, then turning, now sunlit, silver, passing in front of a half moon in the dawn sky. Change your chemistry. A dying custom, plastic manger lit up on the front lawn. She serves as a crossing guard by the schoolyard in the mornings, chain-smoking in her orange reflector vest, accompanied by a black chihuahua. form of the pipe as counterpoint to the shape of the face (his long, white hair half-wild) Chairs upturned upon tables, the cafe is closed. This was history (street numbers broken from the door on the porch). Asleep at the real. Three-sided frame to that woman's walker. December morning, savage in its rhetoric, icy disk of sun striving for a workshop poem effect. A sweep at the veal. A preference for round toothpicks over "flat" ones. Please return trays to the full upright position and fasten your safety belts. Cartoon pig made up as a clown (it starts to rain). Gradually the child's crying recedes, becoming a kind of song. So odd, the deep blue glass of those window panes. Just walking down the street, the cop's body language reflects tension. Chinese windows. The lesson of the moment. Walking in traffic (try to write). The way the cheek-bones stand out when he drags on a cigarette. Phone poles jut out at angles, wires sag. No time flat. I chew on the end of the pen till the plastic grows soft. Sports car wrapped in tarpaulin. Big Mack truck in front of produce market. Too easily, the nail sticks into the wall. Idly chew on mustache. Two fingers and thumb to grip the pen. Black pigeon among bird crumbs. Pulling off one glove, fishing for exact change to board the bus. Under that loose chic fur she's a larger woman than she cares to think (bleached blonde with rouged cheeks). Cigarette tucked over his ear like a pen. Flattened bubble-form, styrofoam cup. Bodies on the bus brush together (no meaning). The brown of the bruise in the banana peel. Old red dumpster, overflowing with cardboard. First Bart of the day is virtually empty. Already cars pass by on the unfinished freeway. The shamrock is perceptible only from the sky. Grass stains on my chin as I inspect this near horizon. The letters on each blade indicate the patent, the message. That you see words here is a trick. I taught myself to read the clouds.

A new paragraph means a new year. Leading to a direct and further perception: taxes. After Christmas, the white backsides of cut-out paper wreaths hang in the grammar school windows. Extrapolate your theory of the not seen. A stone cherub on one knee holds the flowerpot aloft. Parts is parts. Dried rainwater spots the glass. The watercolor of the doe and her offspring, still in a sunlit glade, the nearby brook fringed with ice, the last clumps of a late snow, is aimed at the viewers' vulnerability, the deep sigh evoking not sentiment, but the memory (half-felt) of the loss of a mother's breast. The transparency of the water in the glass magnifies the goldfish. Dawn but a dilution of the dark. Each solution proposed, gone over in detail. Even the rain is a construct. He was his own name, but to whom?

Leaving the house, I go back and check eight times to see if I've left the heat on, but forget my hat. In sandals and wearing a scarf (scarves?) almost like a turban, the small Laotian woman pulls her shopping cart up the hill, walking in the roadway against the traffic. He wore his pants low, belt about the hips, stomach spilling over. A young woman is carrying a box of vanilla wafers into work. A tube into which one rolls up blueprints. Wearing my Walkman, chewing an apple, far, far from the world viewed. Crouching to read the lead story in today's *New York Times,* I sense the muscles in my thighs stretch tight. That jogger at dawn, first light right behind, is no symbol (is). Genre of the old sailor rides the bus. That freshly-shaved right-behind-the-ears just-from-the-barber look. Dreadlocks on her left side, crew cut on her right. Women coming out of mass from the old stone church. Storefront preschool: the infrastructure redefines space.

Imperfect stranger: these swirls of ink form not a bridge but a barrier, the flask contains but cool tea. Sound, piercing the ears, violates reason, the mirror a reverse of the window. What does it mean, that our national food chain is called Safeway? And then went not down to the ships, old image of conquest. Forth to the shed of the 'hiring office' behind the rusting cyclone fence. Pyrex coffee pot filled with roses. Reba's coffin was larger than the hole they'd dug. Mountain of oranges in the window of the produce mart. Mother and daughter wearing matching daypacks. Distrust the transitions. Billboard of a red bag of fries from McDonald's, with the one word message "YIELD." Motorcycles parked upon sidewalks. Lose mind now, ask me how.

Pigs R Us (horsefeathers!). A jeep in the city, just for the image. Jogging in shorts, but with gloves on. If the self is not writing the poem, who will pay its taxes? It's a cold day, but half the people with gloves are carrying, not wearing, them. A punching bag would scrape your knuckles raw without protection. The conceit fit like a wool knit. The desert relocation village was modeled on a grid like an American suburb, while the Wolof-speaking tribe was polygamous, each wife needing a separate hut equidistant from the central home of the husband, so that when the relief agency evaluation team arrived the buildings were empty, the whole site abandoned, the sands beginning to fill the uncared-for houses, the land itself again in control. What hut? But hat — fat bat cat. The intelligible as a category of itself is perfectly sealed. This is not a diary is not an important distinction, but the omission of the "that" is. Verb in the last place (parallel to what?).

A moustache so thick as to shape the face (nose pointed, eyes deep in the skull). The eyes wide and small, each iris brown-green. The ears virtually without a lobe, set high in the skull. Thick high cheeks pointed outward. The upper lip thin, the lower one full, the two narrow in the round face. The forehead a flat plane, its flesh stretched tightly. Mole on the nostril more red than brown. The flesh at the base of the shell-shaped ear pushes it out, away from the head. Lashes so fine and light, almost impossible to see. Dim sum. Cheese platter. At what point did you become a list (small, crescent-shaped scar below the eye). moon on the horizon stares down.

Lineman strapped high near the top of his vertical. The watchband loose, like a bracelet about the narrow wrist. The past converted into history through redaction. Candy-stripe reflecting strips on the back of the truck. That prosody's different from "the truck's back." How dry the peanut butter gets at the bottom of the jar. Don't weep for me, Union Carbide. Odds, but the g is silent. In the kitchen, the lights out, before dawn: out the window, over the roof tops, the faintest glow gives the sky shape. Most faint. Moist font. Don't sleep for me, Metromedia. But first this word from our sponsors.

12 February: today's heat hints of spring. Young woman on her way to work, hair still wet from the shower. Those apartments have no lobby, merely a stairway behind an iron grating. Half-beauty parlor, half-travel agency. Cafe-deli. Video rentals where previously the Chinese laundry was. Long gray cuff of the garbageman's glove. meter "maid" dwarfed by his own three-wheeler. Fruit drinks packaged in small boxes. Sound of glass echoes as it falls into the large empty drum of the garbage truck. Calling, in his inaugural address, for a "second American revolution," President Ronald Reagan today adopted the platform of the RCP. The idea that the world could be experienced by individuals was that culture's biggest myth. Two boys at play for hours in the shadow of a basketball hoop.

Shape is an issue in the poem. The sky virtually white in the hot still air. Even the asphalt seems to shimmer. That the flood of detail itself thwarts reason. Old white pickup in the driveway is missing its hood, blue plastic tarp laid over the engine. Small ceramic animals decorate condo window. Jogging in place, waiting for the light to change. Where that hill slopes too steep to put houses. Gangs of roofers visible on every street. Inhaling, struggling to find air through the muck in my sinuses. Yet to hold the syntax constant that the rest might vary, Denise, fails to acknowledge that hypotaxis itself replicates the logic of power. Arthritis in my big toe, O variable foot. Young black woman in tank top and cutoffs, dreadlocked hair, sits quietly in the shade of the cypress, reviewing her casebook on torts.

A paragraph in every pot. Black leather tie. Pigtail below ragged crewcut. Rabbit comfit. Simple, sad, savage, soft. The idea that he is not Danny Santiago. The idea that I am not (your name here). Old rolodex sky. Humor is the socially accepted mode of rage. The new first baseman's glove was so stiff as to be immobile. I'm on my back, naked, while you roam over me on your hands and knees, kissing, sniffing, biting, licking, sucking, turning and turning, the room barely lit and virtually forgotten, we're so absorbed in the slow, soft rhythms of this play. Control KD to save text. A>

What is remarkable here in the use of Fibonacci (1, 1,2,3, 5, 8,13...n), the numeric relation found most often "in nature," is not any subliminal assertion of the organic, but precisely the opposite, a form entirely arbitrary and artificial, a shape as inexorable and predictive as a glacier, thoroughly distanced from the conflicting "messages" of content. Was he then no more than a response to his historic condition, a reaction against the attitudes of a previous generation, whose poets had divided on the function of equilibrium in conveying the identity between content and form (between "subject" and "object"), speaking only in terms of tradition, for or against, without anyone ever noting (not even Spicer), the tension, the incommensurable, even shocking discrepancies between the two? I wrote this in longhand to make evident to you that even this Brechtian moment of selfdisclosure, this metacommentary, is itself a mere facade. That I is not the author calls into question here only Creeley, leaving us no closer, the gap between us seemingly unbridgeable. Even as my penis (not circumcised) enters your body (not circumscribed) and we begin again this familiar moving, maintaining eye contact, we remain conscious of the distance, indeed even acknowledge it, taking turns, playing roles, aware of the need for gestures of sharing. Thus blood is thicker than semen due to causality. Musical theme from Bugs Bunny. Think of the shape as a sockful of sand pounded repeatedly against your forehead. Why are you reading this poem? Look out the window (but I didn't say which one). No one will concede ever having thought that Mondale stood a chance. We conceive of suffering because we are stuck on the individual, on the universalization of our own subjectivity into a totem for personhood. That doesn't make it any better.

This can be taken several ways. The fist is to hit with. As if pain (proprioception) were the one true response. The guitar left in the sunlight in the window (an appeal to the image) gets warm, the strings expand, going out of tune. That this is a different paragraph is not obvious. A fistful of linebreaks. I sit in a large chair with my legs drawn up, the back of my right knee serving as a desk. Whoever said syntax was total? An idea of islands forms one state. Acquired Immune Deficiency says it all. Public relations is experienced in private. Just try to change the channel. This buzz isn't static, it's the system.

After staying indoors at home four days with a cold, I'm disoriented back outside: the sense is of extreme vulnerability. Half-awake, the sound of a pre-dawn rain. A woman is rubbing balm on her lips. Their parents put up the down payment. Plastic paperclips never rust. Throwing on my raincoat I discover a pocketful of old gum wrappers. Only down in the projects will you find fathers tending young children on a regular basis. The bicycle wobbles, tilting from side to side, slowly pushing up the steep slope. Flaubert's depiction, though highly visual, is not governed by cine-matic tropes. Breathing deeply, listening for a rattle in my lungs. White styrofoam cups, stacked in rows upside down, line the diner's window. The storm served as winter's coda. The infant's small fist felt strong, grip-ping his beard.

From a schoolyard, children's voices echo up a valley. The wind in the wires. Tiny yellow butterflies. A man sits on his front steps, cleaning little white circles from a three-hole punch. Sheets flap in the light breeze. Gulls swirl, over and over, above the valley. From a backyard one dog barks, then others, until the whole hill is yapping and baying, then it dies back. On the porch, cat sleeps in the shade of a cactus. Against this quiet, all the anger I feel still at never having had a father. Now that I have lived 5 days longer than he ever did. Poor hapless brawler. Big white rooster in a too small yard. Pen's point cutting letters into the page.

Emotional windbreak. Sagging fences. The kitchen was a nook. Smell of the wood of that "bench," within which were kept comics, softball bats, gloves. Until I was tall enough to see better, I thought adults hid things in the sink. My grandfather made all of the formal decisions, against which my grandmother wielded the power of the irrational. I learned to read German before I could English, but I've forgotten every last bit of it, danke. By the back corner of the garage, where the earth was soft and damp, three decades of dead pets had been buried. She was angry, always angry, but it was never clear at whom. Uncle Tootie took me aside to tell me that I had a half-brother, mulatto, mongoloid, dead. Now that my own brother has named his son Danny. Leaving the bank parking lot, gun still in hand, Phil saw that the cops were converging from all directions, so turned the weapon on himself. Skip Casey leapt from the bridge. Joe Eggenberger, the mayor's son, murdered Judy Williamson.

Bright red laces hang from empty hiking boots. That slight electrical hum of the clock. Spinning wheel next to a redwood desk. That such a large, billowing sleeping bag could be stuffed into such a small sack. Theta zed. Where's Fred? Little wicker napkin holder. I metaphor on South Street. Steady drip of fog from the pines, their upper branches iced. At dawn, before the clouds moved in, one could see the mountain. Footprints in the snow grown soft and vague overnight. The flock of Japanese tourists seemed befuddled by the wild deer. I hear the laugh of jays, hidden in the trees.

Too sick to hunt for deer, the coyote looked at the small girl, whose father had brought his BMW to a halt by the side of the road that they might get out to watch this tan, foxlike thing, until it began to approach her with a gait that suggested stalking. The mushrooms were breaded and fried. Empty storefront, shelving stacked against the plate glass doors. The hour at which the city's buses fill the streets, the population shifting downtown from the neighborhoods. Mid-March, the red paper 49er window pennants have faded to a pale pink. From the board room atop the Bank of America building one sees not only the city, but the idea of the city. Pinto with four flat tires is parked on the sidewalk. The coyote stops, too sick even to feign chase. It's the same sun the world around. He came to cherish the commute time over the bridge, often his only solitude for the day. The wildness in the dog startled him, the alertness. Life science. The taste of sweetener in the lozenge.

Excerpt from a review quoted as a jacket blurb, attributing only the journal, cleaves that language from its author, lending it the false air of fact. Even as buildings are not solids. Chained to the stop sign and light pole, newsracks cluster at a corner. With shovels, they pat down hot asphalt into the pothole in the road. Or that a mark in space itself become articulate. Their cynicism toward all government is the only defense they know. Nickel D. Random curds. That the military itself becomes a projective fetish. Satellite dish. Young women in long wool coats bought second hand. For Sale signs hand lettered in automobile windows. Most of the language we consume is forced upon us involuntarily.

Silhouette of the garbageman, can upon his back, trudging, sun behind him, toward the hilltop. The air so cold I feel it in my teeth. He pauses, straightening, which is when I notice his chaps. RVs by the park in which whole families have spent this winter. Please not to contact citizen of other planet! Swarm of saxophones: cave of alto mirror. Lips on reed, puff cheeks out. Short, fast, fat shout (shod fist fed shed). Shi'ite, muslims — don't make no image here. Old Wonderbread wrapper used as a lunchsack (the ecstasy of rock without the agony of metal): dip knees to mark rhythm. Red sun visor without the crown, terrycloth wrist brace...cabin of a Mack truck without the bed (objects of the world indict!). Valley lobster, rag mop lap dog, big plastic trash can all cracked and crushed. Asymmetry of the woman in the park, sunbathing with a cast on her leg.

Latina in a lab coat. One sees, looking out of bus windows, a stain smeared along the glass where, exhausted, so many heads have leaned to rest. O sweet Thai peanut sauce. Bus driver muttering half a song. The primary content of this sentence lies in the sound of its words. Laugh lines about the eye. A typology of persons according to how they decorate that shelf which is the back of their toilets. Cat leaps down from the chair and onto the couch, curling, then going back to sleep. Sauce covers the pasta. Imitation Diebenkorn. Bathtub full of tangelos. You could smell the coffee burning. Junipero, voiced 'J.'

Dot command: muscles needed just to push the spine erect, legs braced, feet against straw mat floor. In tense. Analyze the cellblock through code of family. Looking in, see bus as rolling terrarium. The pure products of America are made in Hong Kong. Ransom of kisses showers together. The answer is, there is no answer. Sketchbook used for spreadsheet. Here we reached the motherboard. Lie back and let my tongue do the work. Sabermetrics comes to OuLiPo. Talking, veins in that long neck pulse. Sitting on a wood bench until Your butt goes numb.

Old shutdown storefront now lived in by hippies Man driving a pick-up while pulling a rag wool sweater over his head. Lecard's Stein. Red dumpsters back of the pizzeria. Whom you have never read has sighed. Tinny rock beat leaking from the headphones of that Walkman. Slowly the well dressed old gentleman in the tweed cap on the bus leans forward to let the glob of spit drop in the aisle. She covers her mouth with the napkin to extract small bones from the fish. Four tiny framed paintings of warships decorate a livingroom wall. Better part of a paragraph. Grain reflects: wind weathers woods. Street full of parked cars = industrial waste. You in your blue-green cotton summer suit.

The way milk crates stack outside a corner store. Cardboard boxes of green bananas. The tide of his hair ebbs. Pronunciation of the letter 'H.' Some mornings one feels deep inside one's head, walled in, but on others really "out there," on the surface, brain's raw edge. Recite to yourself, in order, the phone calls to make once you reach the office. Such dark skin for a strawberry blonde. Leather flight jacket on older man, round face thoroughly freckled. Green bags of cement stacked on a flatbed, long truck too large for this part of the city. Young man, shirtless and shoeless in levis, walks down to the stores at dawn, looking to buy day's first pack of cigarettes. 3 stereo blasters on one bus, each bellowing a different brand of funk. Oh silk-flecked summer sport jacket. Two small white-robed nuns at the corner finger their beads.

Renewal notice enclosed. The next generation of writers disappears into private life. That which exists through itself is what is called moaning. Poet, seeking your voice, gargle. Aliens in the form of daypacks accumulate, waiting to achieve critical mass. Swim team. Fingers swell and the knuckles feel puffy. Above, the lineman is strapped to the pole. Hazy sky, blue, blue-white. I gamble, letting the #10 pass, hoping that the 67 will come along so that I'll have to make one less transfer. Guitar growl atop bar band drumbeat. Oh, lune d'Alabama. Spoon of my old trauma.

Paint garage door trim, standing tiptoe on a bucket. Detail wrecks the theory, back alleys present true house fronts. Feet are not symmetrical. Dawn's initiation I get. Silliman too relate I. Heart pounds, thinking I've misplaced this notebook. Trees too differ as to the ideal form of treeness. Now that the chicken's gone. The sight of one's own back is slightly mysterious, islands of freckles. This is not a system. But the history of sentences, encoded here and everywhere, is not forgiving. Imagine the MX as a mode of full stop. Transparent in the sky, high over these houses, playing some small odd stringed folk instrument, the chicken ascends to heaven.

C section. The Chi Squares (barbershop quartet). Statistical significance is not information. Searching for ducks from this double-bind. The el (missing) is not missing. Dark glasses on a cloudy day. You, sloshing almond oil on my dick, rubbing it, say "Now I'm going to let you come." The way a sneeze bubbles to the surface. One cop walks up to the driver's side of the pulled-over Buick, while the other opens her door, standing cautiously behind it, one hand on the radio, the other on her gun. Concrete sidewalk, asphalt road. Big-eyed child stares over his mother's shoulder on the bus, silently watching me write. Only that hawk, looking so small as it sails up against the scrim of gray clouds, gives one the sense of how high the sky. White-haired man, bearded, deep eyes, dressed in black leather.

A man in a wide-brimmed hat is walking, a red-haired dog along the railroad tracks. Fried trout (breaded). Road gang chawing the sidewalk. At this stop the downtown-bound passengers spill off the bus, a cluster of crosstown riders waiting silently for their chance to board. Was what went on in the sentence merely craft? Three Vietnamese school children, wearing daypacks, run at pigeons to set them in flight. Big street cleaning machine wheezes past, driver atop it in a cabin.

I remember the vegematic. Poetics as cluttered as Gem Spa. The burning of Ukes. Neo real. Your reflection in the highway patrolman's sunglasses seems magnified, rounded. Pinhole at the center of styrofoam cup's plastic lid. Wears the same pair of trousers all week long. Houses without setbacks, with electric garage doors, terraced rock gardens sloping down toward the freeway. At 6:30 the donut shop opens, men in windbreakers, JW women in pairs at the doorway, long cloth coats in the fog, silently, cheerlessly displaying copies of *The Watchtower*. Red chard. Down the hill the sun rises above the factories, between the banks of cloud. A jogger, half-sprinting in the drizzle through these wide, lawnless streets, square homes, pastel colors. Small yellow van, new mode of school bus.

The state is not an Other. The shoes (worn canvas loafers) stick out from beneath the sheet in the gutter, one cop pacing off the distance to a now-empty bus, others directing traffic on past. It was an old gym, dusty with resin. I sipped cider at the party and remembered what it felt like to drink. The way the wind burns the eye. Flower of the Bird of Paradise (watercolor on brick office wall). Proceed by addition. The head, devoid of energy, filled with rain. That one feels fever in one's bones, in the muscles of the calf and shoulder. Red spots on a yellow bulb, balloon-like, called ladies' purses — the flowers, fading, flatten. Asa's eyes mime his mother's. In the morning apt to find my shoes anywhere I happened to take them off the night before. Old oak desk.

Colophon's progress. The lineman on the pole leans back, body, wood and safety belt forming a triangle. 9:00 a.m.: there's already a drunk passed out on the bus. For Sale by Owner. Body of the pen too narrow and long to hold comfortably. Little cloud tufts up over the hill. Let us paint a better bird of-paradise. The six functions of poetry: hair on Caruso's chest, cardboard-n-plastic 3-D glasses, q-w-e-r-t, Formula I, when in Roman sublimation, beep beep beep. He parts his hair in the middle, strong jaw jutting forward, making note in public of the flaws of your body. A single idea, properly understood, takes days. A brick on which is imprinted the word "hidden." Sun Yat-Sen. The throat is a thermos that warms the vowels. My head, my hands, my twenty chipped teeth.

Intensifiers of affect, pear-shaped
resume. The edge of fresh
asphalt gives way to dark
gravel. I come not to bury
caesura, but raise you the limit
under the Rent Stabilization Ordinance
allowable (inverse effect). 4-fingered
cartoon hero with ears so
big, bus with its brights on
middle of the day. The evening news
makes you hyper. Make my
danish. Jelly thematics
glaze with meanings
what morning itself
can't offend. An atelier
big as a thimble, above which
parallel *pied a terre*
for two. From here broad vistas
across the lightwell. Phlegmatic
fields. Clouds dim
morning air, red eye's

black dot narrows: big, gray-
haired woman in her fifties
in polyester pantsuit (maroon)
hoses down porch. Please,
whenever possible, network
with affinity clusters — iteration
posed as dundancy, body
gets voiced as limit, floats
in the harbor. Simple strategy:
all-over surface + art gossip
generates response... grainy.
But I don't understand
these nylons. Inn of
the misgiving. Your experience
of the Borofsky retrospective
is not separable (2,417,642)
from your cheap sunglasses
(2,417,644) in their blue plastic case
lost in the museum cafe. "Ick,"
sneers the hip writing major,
"line breaks." I hobble
to the station platform, to wait
for the train. Green tea ice cream
leaves a taste. One consciousness,
under stress, indefensible
with royalties and copyright for all.
Thick fog trims the hilltop
visible from here. Counting squares
(diamond shaped) in a chain link fence.
I dream I'm in a Chinese fish shop
where they're laid out unfrozen,
without packages, on wood tables
except for a pair of large rusting barrels
filled with water, in which float
squid and shrimp. Upstairs,
above the liquor store, was a small
res hotel. New keyboard lacks
cents sign, round to the nearest verb.
Beats plot the line, pausing
marks it. Dark buildup caked
under the thumbnail. This,

this is my very own falsetto,
stock rising above previous quotation,
echoes stammer. Spires tear
sky's belly. Young anorexic
takes up marathon running. If you
can read this, no thanks
to the MLA. Biker's brains
spread out over freeway.
Big toe sez storm's over.
Vowels hoot. Clear plastic
piewrap, empty, drifts in the breeze
over asphalt. Weak chin, round
face, will merge with neck
as you age. A once-lit cigarette
hangs bent from his lips, the tip
is smashed. Zone edition. Comp-
osition by objective. Small children
in school playground (parochial), boys
 in blue sweaters, girls in red. Down
vests with "fishing pockets" popular
in financial district. How was grease?
Burned out about work. That line
(this one) is about repression
as the heart of narrative
which is why we so love it.
Ambulance without a siren. Hands'
flesh dried out
from having washed so many
dishes. Line break here. How
could father have been shallow,
never having been present?
Shadows in the fog in
the harbor: military boats. Street
sweeper, urban tractor
hums past. Wires fan out
from atop each pole, linking
power to houses. Enjambed
by brigands on a
voyage to fetch munchies,
deputy PD in a cowboy hat.
'Angel of service' motif

to new public works building,
aesthetics of direct mail. That
growl in your stomach sours
your breath. Busdriver with
briefcase and thermos. It's a
spectacle alright, these gaudy slides
projected on the white screen of your
pink belly, smiling faces that warp
into the navel wave
from the Great Wall of China.
A fly is dead in the dust on
the porch wall. A rooster
(offstage) crows. History redacts
populations. A generation of
surfers bearing crosses
from their woodies to the beach.
Dear asparagus fern, do you read me?
What does a horse, stock still
but for twitching tail, brown
skinned, thick-veined (that huge
penis), its mane nearly copper,
alone atop that hill, think?
Consider this lawn a text,
that crabgrass its theme. The purple
outer flower of the columbine.
Epaulets of the red
winged blackbird, breeze
in the cypress. That lichen
is intense. I sense only
sound to connect
that sentence to this. Parallel
bars of a ski-rack in
midsummer bicycles mounted upside
down on the rear of that
Porsche. This is a beach town in
the guise of a text. Two
senior citizens are quarreling,
one of them in tears, in
public so the air feels tragic.
Foxtails are so beautiful when
green. You want to make something

of it? One digests oysters
almost before you swallow them, then
the taste lingers. Large yellow bee
butts its head repeatedly
against the pane. Fog meringue
out over the bay. Vacuous
jabber reduced to trope, bulk
of all talk? Cleft at the heart
of each nipple. The 'windows' narrow
on a cardboard box of tomatoes,
produce stacked by the store front.
Phonetic translation from the original
English, say "Bow wow." Punctuation
ornaments base line. Salsa
horn section, part collie. Cat-
egorize birds into swoopy
and flappy. This idea, that
for each line there is only one
proper break, was itself
historically determined. It is
not symmetry which is
the fundamental fact of
any face but
the opposite I want my
empty V. I want my
Maypo. Safe when taken
as directed. (Less filling!
Tastes great!) Income velocity:
divide the Gross National Product
by the sum total of money
available (M1), to find
number of times per annum
each dollar must circulate to
equal the GNP (current
average 6.7). Formalism
is its own remark: Ninja
throwing star. A brown haze
sits out over the water. On
Divisadero, in front of
the Vietnam-France, I turn
toward you, proposing marriage.

Say that with a little more
conviction. Meanings diverge
for different readers, as well
they should! A weed with a purple flower
fills cracks in the walk. Flossing
versus brushing. Your mind feels
stymied, an old song running endlessly
as if on a broken record. You
never even liked the Everly Bros.
That building mimes its own
I-beams. Like a rationed waterfall
the row of white urinals flushed
continuously. That cop pauses
to adjust his gunbelt. Summer
thunder, rare in the west. I'd
best be going now. Levels of
art, layers of lasagna. Mix-n-
match footwear. Futured hence.
Fruit at the bottom. The people
united...will never be
deleted. Ah big calves
jut from miniskirt. Headphones
leaking rhythm track
on bus. Pull in stomach, pull
up pants. New wave fish sauce.
City faces budget gloom. The pause
that represses. Let's privatize
money! Barrio stop subway
platform. Young woman in oversized
men's dress shirt wears bangs. Man in
cotton hooded sweatshirt worn under
leather 'flight' jacket rubs nose
with back of hand. Tri-color
moustache. Years later, aging ex-
big league pitcher George Brunet
still toils in the Mexican League. Detail
conceived as modernist ploy. Black
crewcut modified by long blonde
braid. Lacy half-slip
under see-thru knit. The lips bulge
to accommodate swollen cock,

rhythm of distinct parts, a-
symmetric. Long green sedan
slides into driveway. Diver's arc
high over still pool. Watch water
blossom (equal but opposite). Through
the roof of a burned-out
house...clear blue sky. The stripes
on her jump suit's pocket run
the other direction. Seaton says
he remembers having read Blackburn
he thinks. Taste of lemon-grass
tames the beef. Go-bots in window of
Hunan cuisine. Little white-haired
woman strains, reaching to pull cord
to stop bus. Absence of articles
as index of the poetic. Over the park
kites hover. The warm breeze tugs
on my straw hat. An old white
pickup, which has been blanketed
by carnations, which have begun to die. The word
Sold imposed diagonally over that "For Sale" sign
in front of the white house. A banquet
at which half the women wear
hats (low crowns, broad brimmed), sign
of old money. Major Feinstein. The carpenters
are stripped down to their overalls
already, and it's not even 9:00 a.m.
Saddened by syntax, I lay
on the chairman's desk. The release
of the TWA hostages obliterates
media coverage of the Lesbian-
Day Freedom Day parade. Mr.
Rambo's Neighborhood. French-fried parsley
conveys a tang. Hazy hot
breezeless day. Why bees are
yellow. So many old poets fear
the new because they mapped their careers
out against a previous terrain. Bash my
banana. Runner's knees absorb
concrete's shock. Backside of the earring
holds it to the ear. To imply space

of 'suburban leisure,' fast food stand's
architect turns the longside of
the building to the road (discrete sign
triggers memory of commercial). What
there is to say the world itself
stutters. Bound in leatherette. The smoke
from that dock blaze clings to the
bay. The abuse of clarity
in a waste of tame
writing. Rambo in Dogtown. The girl
at the door (is not a girl, is 20)
stands naked, talking with her boyfriend
on the porch as he inspects the potted
violet for aphids. Plums drop
and start to rot. Prewash
spray spot remover. I thought I
ought to let the vowels out
that I might hear them. Row
of identical towels dries on the line.
Pus where the bee stung rises white.
Aesthetic jihad. Gunrack on the back
window of the pickup. Shopping mall
parkinglot touch football.
Chinese elder in cotton PJs
(Sherlock Holmes pipe and walking
cane) wears a knit cap
plus highschool varsity letter jacket,
shuffling in slippers up the block.
Toyota chinook. Upscale deli. High
grass shimmers in the wind. In exact
depiction. Kit's pieced. Butterfly
shrimp. A pole upon which
to string power lines. Webbed sky
of the city. Black dove. Light
mottled thru the dissolving fog. Butcher's
apron's stains. He's carrying two
briefcases and a gym bag. Sometimes a
back porch is built as if
it was part of the indoors. An old
guy with his bus pass pinned
to the front of his shirt. Gums bleed

between teeth. Neon sign blinking
in pizza parlor window, locked tight
an hour before dawn, bright pink.
Red down vest over rag wool
sweater. Bike chained to street sign,
front wheel missing. Dark interior
in armored car. The mind without cause,
noisome thing. Disposable
poetics. Flower vendor's stall,
green buckets of color. Snugglebumps.
Hockett's thesis is that the phoneme *f*
is just 3,000 years old, demanding
mouths shaped by the dental
consequences of higher agriculture.
The knees are not
an organ of prayer. Clouds
open in slomo vortex
to emit beam of light. Vis-
passana (sit still). This is
constant process. Restaurants use tipping
to suppress wages. Cramp in gut
like fist clinches. What
to write. What's
to be written. Child's innertube pool toy
the form of a bright yellow turtle. Wear red
for contrast on the telly. A street full
of trash cans, empty and toppled, after
the garbage truck's passed. You prefer
Le Menu tv dinners for their little plastic
plates. She's going to work with that
just-out-of-the-shower
look (what it does to their
imaginations). One sees dinettes
up against the glass walls
of condos, topped with cheap
table cloths — and a small vase
for straw flowers. Old white stove
abandoned on the walk. But here
the storefronts for lease are tiny,
trashed out. The backs of tvs
stare from apartment windows. T

shirt, bull shi'ite. The word
surrounded forms a ground for
nothing. Even after flossing
(grit teeth at mirror), the residue
of last night's popcorn — an 'okay' flick
— lodged between gum and
permanent bridge. I lie awake
feeling heart pound from sushi bar's
green tea. Not the white meat
of the kernel, but its husk or shell
still topped with "butter flavor."
This one jogs with his fists unclenched,
actually shaking his wrists. Your head
rests on my chest. I rise
and read Bill Berkson's newest book
until the morning paper hits the porch.
Prosody made that civilization. A spool
of ribbon typing black. A bus
with its brights on shines
through thick fog. Peach pits
in the crevices, the grid
of the walk. We want a new
line break, more visible, more irrational
than anything. From the street, through the front
window I see the light of the yard
coming in through the back. A man
without a car puts a dime (I think
it's a dime) into the parking meter.
Teenage girl wearing long johns
beneath a long plaid skirt. Burned-out
house sits vacant for a year. Diaphragm
as metaphor. Soft frisbee. Roofers' mops,
solid with old tar, next to the black encrusted
buckets. Small shards of a broken
bottle held together by the label.
Juxtaposition of Rock Hudson
and the 'killer' bees. Society itself presents
borderline features, as once, eighty years ago,
hysteria reigned. A nurse uses the pin
to her name tag to dig out the crud
from the rim of her glasses. After dinner

the four of us climb back into the Honda
conscious of choosing different seats. Wild
artichoke, blue-purple flower. Alabaster
chesspersons. Room in shadows,
morning light on a rainy day.
It's not my story. Sudden
silence. Then the fridge
roars on with a shudder. Oh
son of Sam, son of Shem, sharp stick.
Hard edge end rhyme. A basket
of bees beats a casket of fleas.
The flask of tea is tinged
with lemon, sugar crystals
(undissolved) sediment
on the bottom. Flat
as the hand turned palm down,
wrist extended, rocking
back and forth, a response
to your question, "Is this
wise?" Wide girl in
black leather pants, neo-orange
henna, walks proud.
'Jelly' bracelets encase wrist.
This is not my home or mother
nor displacement of any other
impulse. Little sedans
cruise the mall, all candy-colored.
Lunchbag tucked into
desk drawer, the thrill of
chilled water. Excess toner.
When I'm mad at you (as,
at this moment, I would seem
to be), it is not (directly)
your actions to which I
react, but how, rather,
I am put back in touch with
this old permanent storm
within. The dream of weather
fogs. A woman walks uphill
arms folded. In the projects
on a hot night, doors and windows

left open reveal
small yellow rooms (perfectly
boxlike) within. What's apt
to clutter a car's
back seat. Trochee's heave
is its own haze. Flag on tip
of sedan's antenna. Had O'Hara
lived, what then? Dog leashed
to stop sign by bakery door
whimpers. Bruises on a ripe pear.
A team of painters, gathered
like birds on their scaffold, transform
the three storey building from
brown to white. She raises
the t-shirt up over her head, arms
extended, torso exposed. The organization
of letters into a single word
always already presumes the line.
Squats flex your quads. A deeper silence
than the fog-chilled air over the little
pastel row houses in the valley
between freeways is the one in the head
swimming in mucous, fever buffer.
The sound a woman makes
scratching an ankle wrapped
in stocking. The glamour of
nuance. That place you say
you've never seen in the small
of your back where freckles
run together, small speckled
continent. Thermos of
sun tea, smell of
hot baked chicken
rising from a paper sack.
A stick in the sand extends
the hand into language, yet
meanings ebb. In the shed
you say yes. O lemon yellow
Continental Mark V, revving
your unmuffled engine, this little Olds
(a deeper yellow) covets

your parking space. Pigeons
alive in the bowels of the
subway station. Stop light
at freeway entrance. Alf
Landon bruised
in fall from bed. Window
edits sun falling
upon table, upon the objects
on the table. I'm from Youngstown
where the body happily is not
the body, cat in hopeless
search for lap, to which we're
connected by modem or
memory as helicopters sweep plane
in ye olde search and destroy.
A half-circle of chairs, empty,
gathers around the VCR. A young man
has an idea, which then hardens
into the bright, new coin of the realm
developed not in the manner of thought
but of land. The Christmas lights, shut off
but left hanging about the trim
of the house year round, form a chain
like speech, each of which conceals
 its anchor. Chuckanut Drive.
Any clear thought can scare millions. Me,
I'm merely saying that writing might be
like a sponge and a particularly damp one
what with all the dirty dishes that
have passed thru these hands. But maybe
someone, anyone, thinks they've been fed,
nutrition sucked from these empty calories.
Yet justice is not a placebo. My mom,
alone with two kids, returned
to live with her parents, and did
until she was nearly forty. But
to take a position is to offend
a position. Mr Satellite is a little stick
figure with a happy face in a big blue
roadside dish. Let's switch discourses.
Continuity requires suppression. The swans

of the Gobi desert are an imaginative construct
yet nonetheless real. If a poet could talk
we would not understand her. Line break
applies herewith for its step increase.
Red sun over Elliott Bay: between
two soup kitchens and the Men's Hygiene
Center springs a block of new outdoor
cafes along Pioneer Square. One man
in the crane's glass cage can unload
an entire cargo container, boxes that would
stretch, end to end, seven miles long.
Hammock strung between pear trees, a breeze
in the alley. Dear Credence, that words should not
couple is not possible, unlike the artificial
celibacy of pets. He's pretty bipolar
but she keeps him stable. Clothesline's pole
seems about to topple, old red wood.
Sprinkler's excess leaves a pool in
the gutter, thru which cars whoosh.
Vowels of allegiance. Wooden fire escape
seems a precarious concept. We get out at the border
 to wade through customs. A fear of heights
structures an old oedipal conflict. Attack dog charging
throws itself at the link fence. Juniper
tea, herring roe upon kelp, bannock bread dipped
in oolichan grease, with an entree of caribou stew.
Howe Sound: arriving or leaving
the water yields, blue-green dappled, alive
with its weaving of currents (houses
amid fir trees, nestled into the cliffs) —
we rock, carving our own wake. These
are not facts but points in a logic
learned in the living. Old man, your system's toxic.
Irony without relief is its own belief. These islands
(not hidden in the blood) owned by men (not women),
absolute as anything, their roads leading to the shore,
nonetheless shape water. Learn to sing your name
the way a shore bird skims water. I hunt
for vowels. Nor'east of Keats Island but still south
of Anvil, markers like the trail of crumbs
toward a cartographer's reading. Is the waterfall's

cut any cleaner? The body is not
the plan, but the path of its passage,
pure document. Words in sand
fill with tide's water. A family at picnic
waves at the passing train. This must mean what,
to have been rendered in acrylic? Already
we anticipate loss, the end of a journey,
in spite of the tunnels and starless nights.
Lions Gate to Horseshoe Bay. A man in a cafe
leads his small son to the restroom,
passing the culture. Red plastic trays,
food wrapped in foil. Raven is a scavenger
lives in the park. Who is missing? Who
writes the letter I? Camera pans
to the mirror but is not seen. I sit
on a patio in a park, on the bus, in
a plane. The world is not a text
tho we impose one. Robin drunk
on old plums. Cheap signs
in window of used furniture store.
Felt tip talking stick. Skookum
chuck. In the jack pine
spider's web gleams between branches.
Roots like tangled hair grow out
over the cliff face down to the sea.
Clouds out over the coast
backlit by the sun. The way logs
wash up against the sea wall. Two wasps
rend and devour a bee. A bent box
made of cedar. The sun rises
over Fraser Mountain (which is not
a mountain) which to the captains of poetry
or anyone signals time. Houses on the west shore
catch the light. But there are no captains,
the trucks drifting from lane to lane, their cargo
(ourselves) mooing and bleating from the rear.
Here the cat rubs against me, meowing, real
as dry grass. Time itself is a form of fiction
tho demonstrable through fire or any
unilateral process. Pears ripen in summer
when sheet lightning fills the sky. Each poem ends

with the present tense. Crowds move vacantly
through an airport terminal. The afternoon
heats up, smoke souring the indoor air.
The way continuous perspective disperses attention
until you seem to float freely, apart
from your body, attuned instead to the rhythms
of the world, as to the artificial lights
of interior space, subway or mall. Your name
over the intercom entirely without meaning.
Imagine a luggage that walked. Norms calm
form's charm. The cat's lesson is that it's not us.
Stalk to me. Sunflower bends, weary of its own weight.
Don't tell me I'm running to catch the bus! I
avoids rime, the biggest rhyme of all. I
comb my hair and climb the steps to work

OTHER ROOF BOOKS

Andrews, Bruce. **Getting Ready To Have Been Frightened**. 116p. $7.50.

Andrews, Bruce. **R & B.** 32p. $2.50.

Bee, Susan [Laufer]. **The Occurrence of Tune**, text by Charles Bernstein. 9 plates, 24p. $6.

Benson, Steve. **Blue Book**. Copub. with The Figures. 250p. $12.50

Bernstein, Charles. **Controlling Interests**. 88p. $6.

Bernstein, Charles. **Islets/Irritations**. 112p. $9.95.

Bernstein, Charles (editor). **The Politics of Poetic Form**. 246p. $12.95; cloth $21.95.

Brossard, Nicole. **Picture Theory**. 188p. $11.95.

Child, Abigail. **From Solids**. 30p. $3.

Davies, Alan. **Active 24 Hours**. 100p. $5.

Davies, Alan. **Signage**. 184p. $11.

Davies, Alan. **Rave**. 64p. $7.95.

Day, Jean. **A Young Recruit**. 58p. $6.

Dickenson, George-Thérèse. **Transducing**. 175p. $7.50.

Di Palma, Ray. **Raik**. 100p. $9.95.

Dreyer, Lynne. **The White Museum**. 80p. $6.

Edwards, Ken. **Good Science.** 80p. $9.95.

Eigner, Larry. **Areas Lights Heights**. 182p. $12, $22 (cloth).

Estrin, Jerry. **Rome, A Mobile Home.** Copub. with The Figures, O Books, and Potes & Poets. 88p. $9.95.

Gizzi, Michael. **Continental Harmonies**. 92p. $8.95.

Gottlieb, Michael. **Ninety-Six Tears**. 88p. $5.

Grenier, Robert. **A Day at the Beach**. 80p. $6.

Hills, Henry. **Making Money**. 72p. $7.50. VHS videotape $24.95. Book & tape $29.95.

Hunt, Erica. **Local History**. 80 p. $9.95.

Inman, P. **Red Shift**. 64p. $6.

Lazer, Hank. **Doublespace**. 192 p. $12.

Legend. Collaboration by Andrews, Bernstein, DiPalma, McCaffery, and Silliman.
  Copub. with L=A=N=G=U=A=G=E. 250p. $12.

Mac Low, Jackson. **Representative Works: 1938–1985**. 360p. $12.95, $18.95 (cloth).

Mac Low, Jackson. **Twenties**. 112p. $8.95.

McCaffery, Steve. **North of Intention**. 240p. $12.95.

Moriarty, Laura. **Rondeaux**. 107p. $8.

Neilson, Melanie. **Civil Noir**. 96p. $8.95.

Pearson, Ted. **Planetary Gear**. 72p. $8.95.

Perelman, Bob. **Face Value**. 72p. $6.

Perelman, Bob. **Virtual Reality**. 80p. $9.95.

Piombino, Nick, **The Boundary of Blur**. 128p. $13.95

Robinson, Kit. **Balance Sheet.** 112 p. $9.95.

Robinson, Kit. **Ice Cubes**. 96p. $6.

Scalapino, Leslie. **Objects in the Terrifying Tense Longing from Taking Place.** 88p. $9.95.

Seaton, Peter. **The Son Master**. 64p. $4.

Sherry, James. **Popular Fiction**. 84p. $6.

Silliman, Ron. **The New Sentence**. 200p. $10.

Templeton, Fiona. **YOU—The City**. 150p. $11.95.

Ward, Diane. **Relation**. 64p. $7.50.

Watten, Barrett. **Progress**. 122p. $7.50.

Weiner, Hannah. **Little Books/Indians**. 92p. $4.

For ordering or complete catalog write:
SEGUE FOUNDATION, ROOF BOOKS, 303 East 8th Street, New York, NY 10009